AFTERMATH

A POST-APOCALYPTIC DISASTER THRILLER

FAULT LINES
BOOK 3

HARLEY TATE

Cherise McNeil sucked in a deep breath and smoothed down her hair while waiting for the online meeting to begin. The past five days blurred together in her mind—a turbulent sea of crises and panic and devastation. If it weren't for these daily update calls, she wouldn't have a clue how long they'd been working around the clock to dig out from this unimaginable disaster.

The screen turned black for a moment before splitting into four videos. The White House occupied the upper left with Michael Urston, the head of FEMA, grimacing for the camera. "Good morning, everyone. Let's get started."

He quickly ran through the agenda before turning his attention to Cherise. "Ms. McNeil, you're the closest resource on the ground. Give us an update on the water levels. We know the National Weather Service is anticipating flood waters to recede to a manageable level within the next two days, but what are your people seeing on the ground?"

She cleared her throat. "NWS is correct. Places that were underwater as early as yesterday are now mostly dry. We anticipate the ability to send relief crews into the hardest hit areas of Seattle by tomorrow. However —" She pressed her hands together in front of her, almost in prayer. "We have bigger issues at the present time."

"Such as?" Urston flipped a page on his clipboard, searching for some written explanation for her departure from the agenda.

Cherise pressed on. "The level of lawlessness in the major metro areas. It's greater than anticipated."

"She's right." Governor Peters from Washington state interrupted, his blotchy, bloated face looming on the screen. "The cell phone companies have done amazing work in such a limited period of time, activating cell towers, bringing connectivity back to the region." He glanced away from the camera for a moment to something off-screen. "But it's come with an unexpected cost."

"Such as?" The Chairman of the Joint Chiefs of Staff spoke for the first time.

"It seems people are using social media to, well, tip people off, essentially."

"I don't follow."

Cherise chimed in. "There have been multiple instances of people shooting video at relief tents, showing the blankets and cases of food and water, and explaining where they're located. They might be doing it for the right reasons, but others—"

Peters filled the brief silence. "Are using it as a guide. We've had reports of looting and vandalism, volunteers held up at gunpoint for supplies."

"According to my notes," Cherise flipped a page, "four tents have been raided, all overnight when we're operating on a skeleton crew."

"Any casualties?"

"Not at the tents. I've instructed my people to stand down if they are attacked. But the buses are another story."

"Busses?"

She nodded. "There's a lot of chatter on social media that the buses we use to transport refugees to our more robust shelters, that they're actually supply buses, full of food and water. That we aren't giving those supplies to the people on the ground, the ones who need it most. Several have been attacked—usually with rocks and bricks thrown through at the windows. But one—"

She sucked in a deep breath. "One was shot at. The driver swerved to avoid the gunfire and the bus crashed, splitting in two before exploding into flames."

Someone at the White House swore.

"At the present time we can only account for twenty-one of the fifty-two people on the bus. Many died. A few were seriously injured but survived."

The Chairman spoke again. "Governor Peters, what's the response been from local law enforcement? Is there any capacity to provide assistance?"

"According to the local governments my office has contacted, police departments are overwhelmed with call volume and only a quarter of the officers are showing up for duty. Our National Guard is stretched too thin to provide much support."

"Stretched too thin? Why? What are we talking about, exactly?" The President leaned forward, forearms splayed across the conference table. "Lawlessness? Anarchy?"

"Not large-scale, but in pockets, yes." Peters stared directly at the screen. "That's why I asked about Martial Law a few days ago, sir. We need the military on the ground. We need to keep the people safe."

"What about Oregon? Are you seeing the same things, Governor?"

The Governor of Oregon smoothed his wrinkled tie. "I can confirm we've had some issues with looting, yes. But I'm sure once the aid rolls out more comprehensively, the situation will calm."

The President leaned over and spoke to the Chairman too quietly for Cherise to hear. After a few back-and-forths, he turned again to the camera. "Troops are already on the ground at Sea-Tac attempting to bring the airport back online as quickly as possible. Another group is set to mobilize this week. Instead of sending them into the cities to begin recovery efforts, we can reroute several to assist with security."

"Thank you, sir." Peters leaned back in his chair.

"Anything else, Cherise?"

She was happy to have the additional troops, but she

wondered how long it would take for them to arrive. Longer than they wanted, of that she was sure. She shoved the pessimism down. It would help no one. She glanced at the bullet points on the paper in front of her. "The major relief facility in Ellensburg, Washington, is up and running. As of this morning, over thirty thousand people have been processed through the facility."

"What's the capacity?"

"We have beds for five thousand, five hundred for medical."

"And the excess is where?"

"Once people have been checked in, they have forty-eight hours to regroup and seek assistance from our charity and local government partners before being asked to move on."

"Peters?" Urston waited for the governor to respond.

The Governor nodded. "For Washington state residents, all persons without a place to live are given vouchers for hotel lodging in nearby areas. As you can imagine, it's a large influx of people, and many small towns are already overwhelmed. My office estimates we'll need to expand beyond our borders with relocation assistance within the week."

"FEMA is working with the federal government to establish some sort of federal assistance program for the affected individuals. It will take time to implement. Have you reached out to your neighbors?"

"Idaho and Montana are willing to accept our vouchers and are also mobilizing their National Guard troops to provide assistance on the ground."

"Excellent." Urston ran his finger down the page. "Governor Griffin, any updates on your end?"

"We also have a voucher system." He nodded at the screen. "Governor Peters was gracious enough to share his plan. It's streamlined our interactions with other states. Although Oregonians are a resourceful people, we are grateful for the assistance from both the federal government and our neighboring states. It'll be a long road to recovery, but we're confident we'll get there."

"Any update to your initial casualty estimates?"

The Governor's face fell. "Not at the present time."

"Rough guess."

"Higher than anticipated. Due to the volume of tourists on the beaches when the quake hit, we've revised the numbers upward. When I have more concrete information, I'll share."

"All right." Urston ran through the remaining items on the agenda, everything from status updates on the hospital systems, to bridges and roads, to the upcoming weather forecast. At some point, Cherise stopped listening. As the main point of contact on the ground for FEMA in the region, she understood the necessity of her presence on these morning briefings. But a million people on the ground needed her support. Every minute she spent explaining the last twenty-four hours to her boss and the President was a minute she couldn't use.

At last, the men in the White House conference room wrapped up and she left the meeting. The second she closed her computer, a queue of FEMA employees hustled up to her makeshift desk, papers and notes and questions in hand.

She sucked in a deep breath and managed to smile through the fatigue at the man standing first in line. "Hi, Derek."

"Ma'am." The Assistant Director had aged ten years in five days. He leaned over the desk and spread a wrinkled map with hand-drawn notations across the surface. "Here's the updated list of operational relief tents. Green means they've suffered no issues, yellow is minor skirmishes, red is, well—"

"Compromised?"

"Yes."

Cherise exhaled. Only a few green dots remained this morning. Most were yellow. A significant number were red. She chewed on the inside of her cheek. By the time FEMA was no longer needed, her mouth would look like ground-up hamburger.

"As you can see, the attacks have only increased."

"Any additional incidents with buses?"

"Not yet. We've slowed down our transport times, waiting until multiple buses are full before heading to facilities in a convoy. Several Washington National Guard units are now accompanying these convoys to dissuade any attacks."

"Good." Cherise rubbed a thick knot taking up residence in her right shoulder muscle. "Unfortunately, that's probably the best we'll get for the foreseeable future. It doesn't appear additional security will be arriving anytime soon."

"What about the Marine Corps or the Army? I thought—"

"You know how slow they are to mobilize. The Chairman offered to reroute troops from the airport, but none that are already there. Only future mobilizations. He wouldn't give a timeline."

Maybe she should have pushed harder for something concrete, but she was a small fish in a big pond. There were only so many bites at the apple for her. If she used all her capital now, she might miss out when they really needed it.

"Anything else?"

Derek glanced behind him. "Nothing that can't wait for an hour." He nodded at her empty coffee cup. "Need a refill?"

"That would be amazing."

He plucked her cup off the table and flashed a tight smile before heading toward their makeshift canteen. It wasn't much—mostly coffee and water and packaged snacks—but it was better than most of the residents of Seattle and Portland had on offer. The odds of anyone still trapped being alive dwindled every hour at this point. Soon, all their efforts would shift away from rescue and onto recovery.

It would be a long road, but she would see it through. They all would. She managed to brighten as a young woman stepped up to the desk.

The woman pushed her glasses up her nose. "Hi, Ms. McNeil."

"What do you have for me?"

"Got you a Snickers, kiddo." Mika's dad slid the candy bar across the grooves of the picnic table. Early morning sun forced him to squint as he eased onto the bench with a smile.

"Thanks, Dad." She plucked the candy bar off the worn and faded table and peeled down the wrapper before taking a bite, savoring the morsels of chocolate and peanuts. When was the last time she'd eaten more than a snack? The breakfast sandwich before they loaded the helicopter?

It felt like a year ago, not yesterday.

It was hard to focus on anything. She'd thought after a solid night's sleep tucked against her father's large frame on the bus, that she would be fine. But she wasn't.

"Sorry it's not something more substantial." Her father's face creased with worry as he frowned.

She tried to perk up. "It's delicious." Mika made a show of chomping on another bite. Every time she brought her jaw together, the pain radiating through her head intensified and the ringing in her ears increased.

Her dad had asked her repeatedly if she was okay and she'd agreed, brushing off his concerns. Maybe she should have told the truth—that her eyes unfocused every few minutes, that she barely remembered anything that happened yesterday, that her hands trembled if she didn't work to hold them still.

A combination of adrenaline and shock had propelled her through yesterday, out of the little cubby in the destroyed cafe and back to the relief tent and the bus that would take them to her mom. But when they'd been delayed...

Mika shoved down her spiraling thoughts as a woman approached wearing navy scrubs under a pale gray cardigan. She wrapped the sweater snugly around her chest and crossed her arms. "It's freezing out here." She smiled at Mika and her dad. "Hi, I'm Bridget."

Mika tried to concentrate on the stranger. "I'm Mika."

Her dad nudged his chin in acknowledgement as he cracked open a can of soda. "Clint."

Bridget yawned. "Nice to meet you guys. Do you know why we've been here all night?"

Mika's dad nodded. "Bus driver came over the speaker and said he'd been radioed to stop at the first safe place to rest that he came across and to wait for further instruction. Something about a convoy. Didn't say much more."

"Oh." Bridget frowned, rocking on her heels as she

stood beside the picnic table. "Must have been asleep when he said that." She glanced around. "Where are we?"

"On I-90 headed toward Ellensburg. Before Snoqualmie Pass, I think."

"I can't believe we had to stay here overnight." A lanky, clean-shaven man eased onto a picnic table bench one over. He lifted his wire-rimmed glasses and rubbed his eyes. "I'd kill for a cup of coffee."

"No kidding." Bridget hugged her sweater a bit closer around her. "At least there are working bathrooms and stocked vending machines."

"True." The man on the bench ripped open the wrapper of a honey bun and wrinkled his nose as he gave the pastry a sniff and introduced himself as Tom. "So, where you guys from?"

"Outskirts of Seattle," Bridget volunteered. "Lucky to be alive. I was heading for my shift at the hospital when the quake hit. Made it out before the water, thank goodness. How about you?"

"Bellevue. I was at work. Mid-rise on the edge of the financial district. Building was newer so it didn't collapse." He took a tentative bite of the pastry and shoved it in his cheek as he kept talking. "A boat came by after a couple of days. Plucked me off the roof."

They both turned to Mika and her father.

"Clint and Mika," her father offered, pointing at them each in turn. "From Port Angeles."

Bridget sucked in a sharp breath. "How'd it fare?"

"Not well." Her dad sobered and focused on the table.

Mika managed to shove the last bit of the candy bar into her mouth and chew. With her mouth full, she didn't have to answer any questions.

"I can imagine," Bridget said in an empathetic voice.

I severely doubt that. Mika swallowed and leaned forward, cradling her head in her hands. Why did everything have to hurt so badly? Her limbs, her head, even her heart. As soon as she woke up that morning, she knew something was wrong. She didn't feel like herself. It was as if she was wrapped in a ball of cotton wool, separated from the world by a foot of fuzz.

The conversation continued around her, adults sharing war stories about what they saw, felt, endured. She couldn't concentrate. Couldn't keep a hold of any of their words or any consistent train of thought. It was as if everything in her brain had jumbled up together.

Bridget tilted her head to the side and gazed down at Mika. "You feeling okay, hon?"

Bridget's voice sounded like it was coming from the other side of a tunnel. Mika opened her mouth. "I—" The candy bar wrapper dropped from her slackening fingers and landed on the grass under the table.

Her father moved across the table in an instant.

Bridget knelt beside her. "I'm a nurse, sweetie. You mind if I check you out for a second?"

Mika nodded. Her brain was thick and slow as a numb sensation traveled through her muscles.

Her father spoke over her. "She had a bit of an

electric shock yesterday. We were wading through flood water. There must have been a live wire submerged some length in front of us. We were trying to reach the flooded part of Bellevue."

"Why would you do that?" Tom's face wrinkled.

Mika's dad lifted his head and turned to Tom. "Her mother—she's missing. We were looking for her. She worked at a law firm downtown."

Tom exchanged a somber look with Bridget, but neither said a word.

"Mind if I put a hand on your forehead real quick?" Bridget asked Mika.

Mika slowly shook her head. It felt like her brains were soupy and sloshing around inside her skull. She blinked, wondering why she suddenly felt *weaker* after eating the candy bar. Since it was the only thing in her stomach for a long while, maybe it was doing weird things to her.

Bridget's hand was ice cold on Mika's skin, but it was a welcome relief to the warmth moving through Mika's veins.

"She's clammy. A little warm." Bridget looked at Mika's dad. "Did she lose consciousness before? In the water?"

Her dad gripped one hand in the other, squeezing hard. "Yes, for about a minute."

Bridget reached for Mika's wrist and placed her fingers on the inside, feeling for a pulse. She counted to herself for a while. Mika struggled to stay alert.

"Can you look up, Mika?"

She did as requested as Bridget fished her phone from her pocket. She turned on the flashlight and shone it briefly into each of Mika's eyes. "Her pupils respond evenly and her pulse is constant. But without an MRI or other diagnostic testing, I can't rule anything out." She smiled a sort of apology at Mika, as if she had any control over the lack of available medical care.

"Maybe she just needs to rest. Get some sleep perhaps?" Tom suggested, his uplifting voice slicing through the fog in Mika's mind.

Bridget's expression was hard to read. Her eyebrows knitted. "It certainly couldn't hurt. Are you out of sorts at all, hon? Vision blurry?"

Mika's father hovered so close she could feel his hot breath on her cheek. She'd worried him. She pulled back and tucked her hands into the sleeves of her sweatshirt. "Not really. I'm fine, honestly. I think it was just a sugar rush."

"Are you sure? If you're dizzy or feeling confused, you might have some neurological issues. Electrical current can do funny things to your brain."

Her father's breath caught. The last thing Mika wanted was to worry her dad any more. Until they found her mother, she would pretend everything was fine. She forced a smile. "I'm fine. Honest."

Bridget offered a kind and soothing smile. "If you're sure." She glanced at Mika's father. "Just have her checked out when we make it to Ellensburg. To confirm."

He nodded. "Thank you."

"Wish I could do more." Bridget gave Mika's

shoulder a light pat. "Just try to take it easy today. I know the circumstances aren't great. You need a real bed to sleep in, but just don't overdo it. Avoid strenuous activity and chill out. At least for a few days."

"We could all use that advice," Tom offered around another bite of honey bun. "Especially the bed part."

After a few moments of awkward silence, the conversation picked up again between the adults, discussing what each planned to do after reaching the shelter. Mika tried her best to listen, but it was impossible. Her whole body ached. She was bone tired. Using her arm as a makeshift pillow, Mika leaned on the table and closed her eyes.

A rumble woke her some time later. She sat up, rubbing away a dreamless sleep as her father stood, one hand shielding his eyes from the sun. She followed his gaze. A series of trucks, squat and sand-colored, rolled into the parking lot.

Mika's dad eased to his feet. "Looks like the Guard is here."

"Is that who we've been waiting for?"

Behind the National Guard vehicles, two buses like the one they'd all piled into the day before eased into the parking lot. Through the dark tint, Mika made out heads in every window.

"Looks that way."

Bridget frowned. "Why would FEMA make us wait for the National Guard?"

Her father's voice came out measured. "I'm guessing because we need the protection."

Mika stilled. Was something going on? Why would a bus full of natural disaster survivors need protection?

Men in uniform poured out of the first vehicle, one barking orders.

"Dad?"

Her father glanced down at her with a smile. "It'll be fine, sweetie. The Guard will escort us to Ellensburg, we'll get you checked out, and find your mother ASAP."

Mika clung to the hope in his voice. She needed something, anything, to keep her tethered to reality.

CHAPTER THREE

"Everyone who's checked in? Hi, over here!" A young man waved a clipboard high in the air. The red lanyard attached to his FEMA badge stood out against the pale yellow of his T-shirt. "If everyone could assemble over here, please!"

Daphne glanced at Jocelyn. The other woman shook her head in slow motion, braids swinging back and forth across her shoulders. Samuel hung back as well, hands stuffed into his pockets. *Good.* There was solidarity in numbers. Daphne crossed her arms and waited as most other refugees ambled over to the young man.

He smiled out at the little crowd huddled together until his gaze landed on their small trio. His lips slid into a line. "Excuse me, Ladies? Gentleman? I really do need you closer so I don't have to shout."

Begrudgingly, Jocelyn reached for Daphne's arm and gave it a bit of a tug. "Come on."

"I'm not getting on a bus."

"Not saying we are, but we might as well try to be polite."

Daphne let out a rather loud *harumph*, but she complied, easing forward until she stood at the back of the crowd.

"Great." The young man smiled again. "Now that we're all here, I wanted to introduce myself. My name is Michael, and I'm the transportation coordinator today."

Jocelyn leaned close enough to whisper. "I thought he was going to say tour guide."

Daphne snorted.

"I'm happy to report that we have multiple buses available today to take you all directly to our main shelter. I know some of you may be reluctant to board—"

Daphne almost flashed a rude gesture, but she restrained herself.

"But I assure you, with the National Guard now accompanying every bus, the journey is safe and secure." He smiled again and Daphne wanted to punch the look right off his face. "If everyone can head to my right, you can begin lining up, please."

The three of them watched as one-by-one the group dispersed, all heading toward the transportation. Nick lined up with the newcomers, apparently nonplussed by the prospect of riding in another death trap on wheels. It didn't take long for Daphne, Jocelyn, and Samuel to be the only people left. Michael approached with the same out-of-place grin. "Hi, is there a problem?"

Jocelyn raised an eyebrow and palmed her opposite

hip. "Do you not understand what happened to us the last time we loaded onto a FEMA bus?"

Michael closed his eyes for a moment, as if summoning patience from somewhere deep inside himself. When he focused again on Jocelyn, his voice was slow and steady, as if trying to reason with a toddler on the verge of a tantrum. "Ma'am, I can assure you that the new bus is safe."

Jocelyn stared back, nonplussed. "How? How exactly can you assure me?"

"With the Guard—"

"We were *attacked*," Daphne interjected.

Michael opened his mouth to respond, but Jocelyn pointed her index finger, nail scuffed and cracked after losing the acrylic, at his chest. "The bus ripped in two and burned into bits. People died. A *lot* of people."

"Which is why it's in your best interest to get on a new bus." His artificial smile was back, driving Daphne insane. "Going forward, we're only sending buses once a day to the processing facility in a convoy. National Guard troops will be riding on each bus and National Guard vehicles will start and end the convoy. I assure you, the trip is safe."

"What if we decline?" Samuel spoke for the first time.

Michael exhaled in exasperation. "I can't force you onto one of the FEMA buses, but if you choose not to go, you won't be guaranteed access to the refugee area. Our main shelter facility in Ellensburg is the processing area for all relief. There will be food, shelter, and supplies.

Resources to help you secure temporary housing and medical care. If you don't go to the shelter, you'll be on your own."

Daphne stilled. Her husband and daughter were on the clipboard she'd seen at the tent. Presumably, they had boarded one of the other buses the day before and were now at the shelter, trying to find her. If she didn't get on a bus, would she find them? But if she did and something happened...

A shiver of dread snaked down her spine. She couldn't do it. It didn't matter if the bus guaranteed access. She would find another way. "Are you sure we can't access the shelter without taking a bus?"

Michael hesitated. "I—I'm not sure to be honest. But I know the bus is a guarantee."

His non-answer all but sealed the deal for Daphne. She turned to her new friends, hoping they shared her reluctance.

Samuel picked up on her concern and caught the attention of the FEMA employee. "Michael, is it?"

The man nodded.

"Can you give us a few minutes?" Michael opened his mouth to argue, but Samuel kept talking. "Seems the least you can do seeing as we managed to find this tent again and alert you to the survivors from the crash."

Michael held up his hands in surrender. "Fine. But the buses are rolling out in the next thirty minutes."

Samuel waited for the FEMA employee to be out of earshot before he spoke. "Looks like we have two options.

One, we get on the bus and hope we don't turn into a human barbecue on the highway."

Jocelyn crossed her arms in disapproval.

"Two, we figure out some other way to reach Ellensburg."

"Are we sure we even want to go there?"

Samuel's cheeks lifted as he thought over Jocelyn's question. "I think we do. Not only do they have food and at least rudimentary shelter, they mentioned longer-term aid. When I was helping earlier, explaining where the bus crashed to some of the other workers, they mentioned that over ten thousand people have already been processed through that facility."

"Ten thousand?" Daphne blinked. "I don't know if I should be surprised it's that high or that low."

Samuel nodded in agreement. "They said the federal government is working with the states to provide some sort of voucher system. That we can stay in hotels free of charge for a certain amount of time."

"But?"

"We have to go through the FEMA registration to do it."

Jocelyn sagged. "So we don't have a choice."

Daphne spoke up. "I don't, that's for sure. If Clint and Mika are at that shelter, then that's where I need to be." She glanced over at the buses lined up in the distance. "Maybe Michael is right. Maybe we should just get on a bus and pray we don't crash."

"No. No way." Jocelyn shook her head. "If you want

to, that's fine, but I'm not getting anywhere near one of those blue and white death traps."

Samuel glanced around before lowering his voice. "I'm not keen on the bus angle, either. But we need transportation."

"We're listening." Jocelyn focused her gaze on him.

"I'm guessing most of the cars around here are flooded out, but there's got to be a few that still turn over. If we can find one old enough, I should be able to hot wire it. Get us out of here."

"You want us to steal a car?"

He rubbed at an invisible spot on his cheek. "I'm guessing no one's going to miss a clunker that's been abandoned for the last six days, do you?"

"What if we get caught?"

Jocelyn raised both her eyebrows this time. "You really think the cops are gonna ask for our license and registration in the middle of all this? Girl, you're even crazier than I thought."

Daphne snorted out a laugh. "I suppose you're right."

"Mm-hmm," Jocelyn agreed. "Don't you know it."

"So how do we do this?"

Samuel glanced around again. "We walk away. Simple as that. If they aren't physically detaining us, then they won't stop us. We can head toward dry land, streets that don't have any signs of past flooding. We can't be that far."

The weight in Daphne's chest eased. Maybe this would all work out. Away from FEMA employees, away from all the other frustrated, hurt, and worried people, maybe they could make faster time. Better progress.

Without another moment's delay, the trio picked their way around the last of the other refugees assembling in lines and headed toward the road. As soon as Daphne's foot contacted the pavement, she winced. Black dirt and grime and unmentionable horrors clung to the bottom of her bare feet. If she didn't already have an infection from bacteria entering any open wounds she'd suffered, she would soon.

All three of them smelled. Daphne by far the worst. At this point, she'd almost internalized the noxious combination of sewer and rot and salt water. Her hair hung in ratty clumps, dried flood water crusting between her once-blonde waves. She refused to even look at her clothes beneath the blanket still wrapped around her shoulders.

"Be careful not to step on anything sharp." Samuel cut through her thoughts.

Daphne blinked at him, nodded.

"My shoulder doesn't feel right. I think I jammed it in the crash." Jocelyn frowned and rubbed the joint with her thumb.

"I'm sore too." Every muscle in Daphne's body ached in protest as if it was too battered to take another step. Her thighs burned. Her shins tingled and her knees threatened to buckle. "My back is killing me."

"With any luck we'll be in a car soon, and everyone can take a load off." Samuel plowed ahead, searching for a suitable vehicle.

Daphne sighed with relief. She was in good company. She just had to keep reminding herself of that.

After a few blocks of trudging along, Jocelyn placed one hand against the wall of a brick building and paused. "Sorry guys, I need a minute."

Daphne stroked her back. "Don't apologize. We can stop if you need to."

The air conditioned, cloth seats of the bus sounded more favorable to Daphne now. Maybe they'd made the wrong decision.

A few paces in front of them, Samuel glanced back, but pointed forward. "I'm just going to check out around the corner. See what's up ahead."

Daphne's throat clenched as she watched him disappear. After a minute or two, Jocelyn pushed off the wall.

"You good?"

Jocelyn wiped her forehead with the back of her hand. Smudges of grit and dirt remained. "I think so. Let's go. I don't want to make Samuel wait."

They hobbled forward. Samuel was already inside a vehicle, an older low-slung sedan parked on the edge of the road, attempting to start it. As they approached, he flung open the driver's side door and stepped out.

"No luck?"

"Flooded, most likely."

"We'll find another," Daphne suggested, trying to boost morale.

"We need somewhere higher up or further ahead."

"What about there?" Jocelyn pointed. The familiar P

in a circle stood out against the black of the building facade. From their vantage point, the deck appeared intact. Although a crack ran through the concrete entrance, it hadn't collapsed. The building beside it suffered more, but it looked passable. Promising, even.

It took longer than expected to make it up to a dry floor of the deck with no signs of water damage. They passed car after car, all too new for Samuel's expertise. At last, they came upon an older SUV, one with a traditional gear shift jutting out from the steering column.

Daphne stopped in front of it first. "This could work."

Samuel cupped his hands over his eyes and peered in through the window. "The gas needle is on empty."

Jocelyn groaned, the echo of her despair bouncing off the walls.

"Let's keep going." Daphne took Jocelyn's hand, marched her upward.

On the next floor, they stopped in front of a truck.

Jocelyn frowned. "It's a little banged up."

"It looks like it was in a side-long collision," Samuel agreed, "but that shouldn't affect the engine." He reached for the door handle and the door swung open, unlocked. He flashed a grin. "Let's hope the luck holds."

He eased into the driver's seat and reached beneath the steering wheel, pulling at wires. Daphne held her breath. Nervous sweat beaded on her skin. If this didn't work, she didn't know how much longer she could walk through the city. The engine clicked once, twice. Daphne crossed her fingers.

At last, it rumbled to life and Samuel let out a whoop of success. "It's got gas in it," he confirmed, pressing his foot to the pedal. The engine hummed in response. "Purrs real nice, too. Let's get going before it changes its mind and stalls out."

Daphne crawled in after Jocelyn. Samuel took the wheel and shoved it into reverse. The break lights lit up the back wall in a glowing red.

Jocelyn's whole face lit up in a relieved smile. "Now all we have to do is get out of here without anything else going wrong."

Daphne looked out the window and chewed on her bottom lip, praying that for once, they'd have an unhindered path ahead.

CHAPTER FOUR
CLINT

"Attention!" A guardsman hollered loud enough for conversation to still. "Everyone waiting to depart, form a straight line behind Corporal Clemens!" He pointed with his free hand at a younger member of the National Guard standing in a clear patch of grass.

Confusing glances darted across the picnic tables.

Tom stood from his bench, pushing the center of his glasses up the bridge of his nose. Beside him, Bridget took an apprehensive step forward. Clint reached out and placed a hand on Mika's arm. They didn't move.

"What's going on?" A dark-skinned man from the group spoke up as he rose from his seat.

The guardsman in charge ignored him. "Everyone line up! The quicker we do this, the quicker we'll be on the move."

Clint glanced around for any sign of the bus driver. At last, he spotted him, head bent in conversation with another man in uniform. He pointed at the road and the man in uniform shook his head. The driver's shoulders rose and fell once before he turned toward the bus and climbed aboard.

About half of the people waiting had followed the guardsman's orders, filing into a single file line in front of Corporal Clemens. As Clint watched, each person was checked one at a time, bags opened, bodies patted down. A wave of frustration rolled through Clint. What did they think was going on here, exactly? These people had escaped a colossal disaster. They weren't criminals.

He glanced again at the bus. Two National Guard soldiers stood beside it, one on each side of the loading door, rifles pointed at the ground, trigger finger straight and clear. They might technically not be ready to shoot, but he wondered what the point of it all could possibly be. Had someone hijacked a bus? Had the shelter suffered some sort of attack?

Worried thoughts about Daphne formed in his mind, each scenario more outlandish than the next. A mass riot at the shelter when food or water ran out. A drug cartel breaking in and taking over. A bus of angry, hungry people on a collision course with the triage tent.

He shook his head. He needed more information before he took a single step onto that bus. "Head over to the bathroom, okay? If anyone asks, say you need to go before you get on the bus."

Mika lifted an eyebrow in obvious confusion. "Why?"

Clint cast a quick glance at the line. Twenty people deep, it would take a few minutes to clear. "I'd like to know what we're getting into, that's all. Meet back here in five."

"O—kay." Mika pushed off the bench and walked slowly toward the restrooms.

Clint surveyed his options. The two guardsmen at the bus were out. So were the two checking bags and maintaining order in the line. The one in charge was visibly irritated already, waving his free hand at the stragglers and encouraging them to hurry.

Finally, he spotted someone promising. Over to the side, a small group of men in uniform waited. One blew a puff of smoke into the air. He headed toward them as quickly as possible without drawing unwanted attention. As he neared, one turned toward him and the hand holding his rifle twitched.

Clint held up both hands in front of his chest to show he meant no harm. "Hey fellas, I'm wondering if you all know what's happening. Is there some problem at the shelter? No one's told us anything."

The guardsmen all traded looks. The one with the cigarette took one last drag before dropping it on the ground and crushing the burning stub with his heel. "Don't know much. Just that we've got to guard the buses from here on out."

"Guard them?" Clint's mouth fell slack. "Did something happen?"

Another man in the group lifted a shoulder. "Heard something about an ambush, maybe. Don't know specifics. They don't tell us much. Just where to go, what to do."

Clint's mind reeled. An ambush? What if Daphne—? The group began to break apart, some men heading back to their vehicles, another moving toward the buses. "Please, do you know anything else? Was everyone on board killed? Were there survivors? Are they at the shelter?"

"Look man, we've got to go. Lieutenant Jansen'll have our necks in a minute."

"Please—"

One by one, each guardsman ignored him, heading to their assigned locations.

"Sir! Sir, is there a problem?"

Clint turned to find the man in charge barreling toward him. He held up both hands again. "No, no problem. Just trying to find out information about the ambush. My wife—"

The guardsman shook his head. "I'm not at liberty to provide any information at this time. Our orders are clear. Inspect all passengers, get them on the bus, and roll out."

"But—"

"Are you going to be a problem?"

"No."

"Then get in line."

Clint turned toward the bathrooms. "My daughter—"

"Sir?" The man's rifle moved in his hands.

Clint held his breath for a long moment. At last, the door to the restroom opened and Mika emerged. He exhaled. "Sorry to be a bother." He held up one hand again in apology and made his way toward the dwindling line. He met Mika at the rear.

"Everything okay?" She glanced between him and the man who'd blown him off. He still eyed them both with suspicion.

Clint smiled and rubbed her back briefly. "Everything's fine. Ready to load the bus?"

She stared up at him for a long moment before nodding. "At least the seats are comfortable. And there's air conditioning."

Clint *mm-hmmed* in agreement and ushered his daughter toward the guardsmen inspecting the passengers. He held his breath as a female national guard soldier looked Mika up and down, patted her waist and the bottom of her legs. He sighed with relief once the woman finished and waved Mika along.

He gave his daughter another smile. "Just try to get some sleep once you get on the bus. And save me a seat."

She nodded over her shoulder at him before heading toward the bus, although her forehead creased with worry and skepticism.

Clint approached the male guardsman. He stood like a tower, his expression stern, eyes scowling, cheekbones and jawline hard.

"Stand here," he told Clint, pointing to an empty space in front of him.

Clint did as he was told. Sprawling fingers spread out across his torso and down his legs.

"You're good to go." The soldier dismissively nudged his chin toward the bus.

As he climbed the steps, Clint debated on whether to tell Mika about the ambush. He leaned toward telling the truth, arming her with the knowledge of potential disaster, until her pale face came into view, hovering above the seat backs. Her sunken cheekbones and hollow eyes telegraphed the strain of the past week. She'd already been through enough physical and emotional torment to last a lifetime. She didn't need to worry about her mother right now. She needed to rest.

"Hey, sweetheart." He smiled at her and slid into the seat next to her.

Her eyes fixed on him, wide with worry. "Everything alright?"

"So far," Clint managed, then gave her a wry smile. "I thought I told you to get some sleep?"

Mika sighed. "I'll sleep. Eventually." She turned to stare out the window, tucking her legs up underneath her and resting her head on the corner of the seat and the sidewall of the bus.

Clint stared straight ahead, watching the last handful of refugees climb on board. Behind them, three National Guardsmen followed, rifles pointed toward the floor. They took up positions evenly dispersed throughout the bus, one at the rear, one in the middle three rows in front of Clint and Mika, and one behind the driver.

Within minutes, the bus shimmied and began to roll forward. Two Humvees moved out first, followed by the other two buses, and finally theirs. Behind them, the remaining military vehicles followed. They were in a guarded convoy.

Clint glanced at his daughter. He hoped for her sake this was all unnecessary. But he doubted it. A show of force this large only meant one thing. They were headed for trouble.

The truck engine idled, the nose of the hood sticking out of the exit of the parking garage. Samuel flicked his head first one direction and then the other. He pointed a thumb to the left. "We're gonna have to go that way."

Daphne's heart nosedived.

Jocelyn twisted in the seat. "But that's the way we came."

"Yeah, but it's also east." He pointed back to the right. "The flooding will be worse to the west and we'll probably end up trapped in the disaster zone."

Jocelyn groaned and worried her hands. "Alright, but can we at least try to avoid the FEMA tent?"

"I'll do my best." Samuel flicked the blinker and pulled out cautiously onto the street. They were the only moving vehicle on the road. Muck and debris and abandoned cars slowed their progress. The speedometer hovered between fifteen and twenty.

Daphne pressed her knees together. A huge neon

sign might as well flash above the vehicle, they were that conspicuous. If the bus was a target, what were they? She chewed on the inside of her cheek.

The truck hummed on, approaching the FEMA tent. She clenched her jaw, anticipating commotion or a series of shouts. A sour churn roiled her stomach.

Jocelyn slunk into her seat and put her hand over her face. "What if they recognize us?"

"Sun's hitting the hood." Samuel turned the wheel. "They can't make us out."

"Oh yeah? Have you seen yourself and that scratchy beard?"

Samuel's upper lip twitched until it cracked into a smile. He shook his head, giving her a sidelong glance. "You're something else, you know that?"

Jocelyn tossed him an innocent shrug. "I may have been told that once or twice in my life."

Daphne suppressed an amused smirk. At least they were all keeping it together.

"Alright, here we go." Samuel gripped the steering wheel tighter.

Jocelyn sunk lower into her seat, her breath coming faster. Daphne found herself reaching for Jocelyn's hand, lacing their fingers together and squeezing. Samuel stiffened, but he kept his eyes on the road. They edged past the FEMA tent. A few faces peered at the truck with curiosity, but no one stopped them.

Once the tent grew small in the rearview mirror, Daphne exhaled a deep breath she hadn't realized she'd been holding. "We made it." She eased her hand out of Jocelyn's, wiping the clamminess on her pants.

They eased down the road, Samuel doing his best to avoid debris as they made their way out of the worst of the flood-damaged areas and onto dry streets free from sludge. No more than five minutes passed before the first signs of trouble emerged from a side street. Three men and two women, all bedraggled and exhausted, with limp gaits and hunched shoulders ambled onto the road.

Only one—a woman whose hair might have been blonde, Daphne couldn't tell thanks to the dirt and grime clumping the strands—wore shoes. The other woman limped a few paces behind, a dusty backpack clinging to her bent back.

One of the men's head jerked at the sound of the truck's engine. Jocelyn stiffened beside Daphne.

"Try to go around them." Daphne grimaced and clenched a fist in apprehension.

"Hey, where'd you get that truck?" One of the other men shouted, he lunged forward, arms extended, fingers grasping for the back bumper.

Samuel eased the truck past them, not slowing down.

"Stop!" One of the women called out. "Come back!"

Daphne squeezed her eyes shut, torn between wanting to keep going, and wanting to stop.

"We don't have room in the cab." Samuel made the decision for them. "If they rode in the back, they'd kill our gas mileage. We barely have enough to make it to Ellensburg."

After a minute, the voices petered out behind them.

Daphne forced her body to stay straight and not turn around. It pained her not to help, to turn a blind eye to people in obvious distress, just like she'd been these past days. But Samuel wasn't wrong.

Did that make him right?

Silence swallowed the three of them, the rumble of the truck's engine the only sound as they kept driving. Daphne craned her neck and stared out at the midday sky. Clouds clung to the tops of the still-standing buildings, but above them, the sun glared almost in judgment. Guilt clogged her throat and she coughed.

They kept driving east and south, aiming to connect with I-90 and hopefully clearer roadways. Daphne stared out the windshield, eyes unfocused as she thought about everything she'd been through and all the people in the metro area still suffering. She was dirty and exhausted. Hungry and in pain. But she was alive. No broken bones. Nothing more than superficial injuries and emotional scars.

They neared a sign for I-90 and hope percolated in her chest. Maybe they would make it without issue. Samuel eased toward the on-ramp when Jocelyn spoke up.

"Guys?" Her voice warbled.

Daphne blinked and turned in the direction the other woman pointed. *Oh, no.* On the on-ramp, practically blocking the entire road, a larger group of people walked. Some carried bags, one a crate stuffed high with belongings, another a small child piggyback.

"Should we—"

"If there were too many before, there's definitely too many now," Jocelyn answered. "We'll be swallowed up."

Samuel tightened his grip on the steering wheel and pulled himself up straighter in the seat. "I'll try to edge by."

"Maybe we should go around," Daphne offered. "Go underneath the highway and find another route."

"Ninety's the best way from here," Jocelyn argued. "Everything south is what, residential?"

"Wouldn't that be safer?"

"Not if we end up trapped on a side street or stuck in a cul-de-sac. If we keep heading south, we'll end up in Cougar Mountain. We'll either have to go all the way around or come back here."

Daphne swallowed. Maybe Jocelyn was right, but she had a bad feeling about it. She glanced at Samuel. "Try it, I guess."

He nodded and pressed the gas, heading toward the crowd. It didn't take long for all three of them to realize their mistake. Not only were there more people than they anticipated, but they obviously were there on purpose, attempting to stop vehicles from entering the highway.

Men fanned out across the road as they approached, each one holding up his arms in an X.

"They aren't going to let us through."

"Why not?" Jocelyn's voice cracked with panic. "What can they possibly want from us?"

"Anything they can get." Samuel slowed to a stop before shifting into reverse. "Daphne's right. This is suicide."

As soon as the truck began to turn, the crowd did as well, upraised arms turning into fists. Legs pumping, shouting spreading, the crowd dispersed. A wall of humanity, headed straight for them.

"Samuel?" Daphne managed to shove all her fears into the man's name.

"I'm gonna have to floor it."

"Do it." Jocelyn gripped the side of the door.

Daphne turned around and braced herself on the seat back, watching.

Two men neared the truck, arms outstretched.

The engine roared to life as Samuel dug his foot into the pedal. A man's hand flew out, fingers dipping over the tailgate. He grabbed the lip as he ran, legs pumping as he struggled to maintain purchase.

Jocelyn shrieked beside Daphne and she twisted to see a man reaching for the side mirror, his scraggly hair blown back as he sprinted alongside the truck. His fingers swiped the rusted metal, but Samuel bumped up and over the curb at speed, knocking the man back. The truck's rear launched briefly into the air and came back down hard, jostling everyone inside the cab.

The man couldn't hold on, the last of his strength fading as the truck increased speed. His fingers slipped. He fell to the ground. Daphne closed her eyes. She didn't trust herself not to cry

After a few minutes, Samuel spoke. His voice was quiet and strained. "We'll have to skirt the state parks. Go south around Cougar Mountain, try to make it to State

Route 18. If we can make it that far, I can get us to Ellensburg off the main roads."

Daphne opened her eyes. "How?"

He gave her a small, almost pained smile. "Used to hunt that whole area years ago. Not so many rules back then."

"And now?"

He shrugged. "The timber companies are pickier about who goes on their property. Tacoma limits hunts in a good portion of the area. It all became a bit of a drag for an old timer, to be honest."

Jocelyn leaned forward. "But you can still navigate it?"

"Should be able to." Samuel nodded. "There's logging and forest service roads that crisscross the whole area. Even if we end up stuck on one, we should be able to find another without too much trouble."

Daphne stared out at the road ahead of them. She would trade the prospect of another group of desperate people for trees and elk any day. She gave Samuel a smile. "I say we go for it. What's the worst that could happen?"

CHAPTER SIX
MIKA

Afternoon sun cast a shadow across Mika's lap as it cut through the windows of the bus. A loud hum vibrated through the floor and the seats and Mika's muscles. Something shuddered and she woke with a start, blinking away her confusion.

The bus. *Right.* She sat up in the seat. Ahead, an armed member of the Washington National Guard stood in the aisle, legs braced wide, head on swivel. Another stood mirror image in the rear. Her dad didn't seem to care that an armed escort accompanied them on the journey, so Mika tried to not let it bother her. But the sight of armed soldiers standing guard made her wary.

Outside, one of their vehicles flanked the bus, keeping pace. She assumed the others were either in front or behind. With a weak breath, she turned away from the window and tried to stretch her legs. Pinpricks tingled across her feet and up her calves. She needed to walk, stretch out, sleep in a real bed and not the cramped fabric seat of a coach bus.

Ever since the electrical current coursed through the water and her body, she'd been unable to think clearly. Unable to really feel like herself. All her thoughts came slow, like each word swam through a vat of semi-firm Jell-O to form a sentence.

She tried again to suck in a deep breath, but her lungs refused to hold the air, compressing too soon after the inhale. Numbness tingled in her fingertips. The muscles in her back and legs cramped on and off. Her stomach clenched and released as if a fist held it tight. No matter what she tried, she couldn't shake the effects of the electric current. Was this how it would be from now on? Her body refusing to do that which she used to take for granted? Her brain thick with sludge?

Mika eyed her father sitting beside her. He leaned back, eyes closed, body still. She didn't want to wake him. She had to be strong not only for herself, but for him, too. If he knew she was barely holding on, he'd insist they stop searching for her mom, go to a hospital. Mika refused to consider it. Once they found her mother, they could get checked out. Everything would be okay.

A blue interstate sign for I-90 whipped past the window. How long had she slept? Judging by the sun, a good number of hours. She ran her fingers over her eyebrows, gingerly pressing the pressure points surrounding her eye sockets. Her mother had taught her the technique—a way to alleviate stress and tension instead of taking a pill. It didn't always work, but Mika repeated the procedure anyway, rubbing her thumbs in small circles until the repetition calmed her entire body.

She closed her eyes, about to slip back into sleep, when the bus began to slow. Her father shifted beside her and she opened her eyes.

He leaned across her to look out the window. "Any idea why we're stopping?"

"No." She followed his gaze. "But the—what is it called—a Humvee?"

Her father nodded.

"The Humvee isn't beside us anymore. Every time I looked before, it was there."

Her dad craned his neck into the aisle just as a woman sitting in the row across did the same.

"Any idea what's going on?" She made fretful eye contact with him.

Her dad shrugged.

"Landslide debris up ahead," Tom called out as he rose from a few seats ahead and across the aisle, hooking one arm over the back of his seat. He motioned to the front of the bus. "Looks like the whole side of the mountain collapsed."

The bus engine groaned and the soldier standing at the front shifted uncomfortably from foot to foot. Mika stiffened. She'd heard that type of noise before when the Girl Scout van struggled to make it up the incline while the entire world shook apart.

Her pulse picked up speed, blood whoosh-whooshing through her ears as she tucked her legs beneath her and rose onto her knees to catch a better view. Up front, the bus driver motioned for the soldier to come closer. The soldier nodded at the others positioned further back in the bus before stepping toward the driver.

Something crackled. He pulled a radio from his belt and held it to his ear, listening. A moment later, he responded, pressing the button before speaking. Mika leaned closer.

"Can you hear what they're saying?"

Her father waved at her to be quiet and Mika pressed her lips together to quell her rising unease.

The bus slowed to a crawl. Outside her window, the shoulder of the road narrowed. Rocks, dirt, tree roots and debris littered the side of the road. Branches stuck out from bogs of mud. An exit sign lay bent and twisted across a lane. Mika tilted her head to read it.

Exit 52
W. Summit
1 Mile

She tapped her father on the shoulder and pointed to the sign.

After a moment, he nodded. "We're almost to Snoqualmie Pass. This whole section of highway was cut into the mountain. Remember the concrete retaining wall and all those rocks held back with wire mesh? I'm guessing they didn't withstand the quake."

That's exactly what it looked like out the window. Mika peered closer, cupping her hand around her eyes to shield them from the afternoon sun. Sure enough, bits of metal mesh poked out here and there from the rocks and dirt, with larger hunks of concrete jumbled and jagged all over splayed across the ground.

The bus eased over to the far left lane, a slim Jersey barrier separating it from the drop off on the left. The brakes whined and a minute later, the bus halted, engine idling.

Mika swallowed.

"It looks like the embankment is gone," her dad explained. "The traffic is squeezed to one lane. We're going to have to wait our turn."

She eased back down and tucked her hands beneath her to keep from fidgeting. All of this was way too familiar. The steep incline of the road as it wove its way through the pass. The landslide liquefying the ground. The panic simmering in her belly.

She breathed in and swore she caught a whiff of spent, hot brakes.

The bus fell eerily silent. When the soldier's radio crackled, Mika jumped. The man held it to his ear. All at once, his demeanor changed. He shoved the radio back onto his belt and hoisted up his rifle. He turned to the rear of the bus and motioned with his free arm fully extended, a back and forth motion, palm to the front.

"Dad?"

He shushed her.

The other two guardsmen on the bus moved into the aisle. The one at the front closed his hand into a fist before opening it and holding up what looked like a peace sign. Mika had no idea what was going on. He was signaling something, but what?

As the guardsman up front began to wave his extended arm in an upright circle, the two in the rear of the bus hurried forward.

Someone a few rows up gasped.

"Dad, what is it?" Mika tugged on his arm.

Another rider sat up in his seat, pointing out the window. "I see movement in the woods. Down the embankment."

Mika rose to see, but her father grabbed her and pulled her back down. "Don't make yourself a target."

"A target?" She scrunched up her face. "For what?"

Her father wrapped a protective arm around her. "For whoever's just come out of the trees."

Mika shuddered in alarm. Was this why the National Guard was on the bus? Were they about to be attacked?

A voice rose from outside, distorted from what sounded like a bullhorn. "Everyone remain calm. We're not here to hurt you, we're just here to stop your progress."

"What?"

"What's that mean?"

"What's going on?"

A chorus of questions rose from the bus as people crammed the windows attempting to catch a glimpse. Their hulking, shifting shapes blocked the windows. Mika couldn't see a thing.

Up ahead, Tom claimed a prime view from his side of the bus. He waved to get anyone's attention on the opposite side. "I can see! There's a group of people, men mostly, it looks like. They're armed. Long guns, maybe shotguns, I don't know."

"What do they want?" Mika's dad called out.

Tom twisted around, eyes squinting until he spotted Clint. "They're blocking the road like it's a protest."

Someone groaned. "Protest of what? We're just trying to get to a shelter."

Someone else hollered from closer to the front. "I think that's the point."

Chatter picked up around them, drowning out Tom's attempts to keep talking. It made no sense. Mika turned to her dad to ask more questions, but he was out of his seat, heading toward the front of the bus. He made it halfway before one of the soldiers held up a hand.

They exchanged words. Her father gestured toward the door. The soldier shook his head. His rifle jerked in his hands.

The voice over the bullhorn spoke again. "We're sorry but the pass is closed to all people from the cities. No relief buses are allowed."

What? It made no sense. Why were these people trying to keep them out? She found her father, squeezed in beside Tom, staring out the window. After the voice outside cut off, he returned to their seats. She stared up at him, demanding answers.

He lifted his ball cap and ran a hand over his hair. "It's a group of protestors. Pretty substantial. All armed. They claim the people from the cities are taking over their small towns. Eating them out of food, draining all the gas, taking over the hotels and the sides of the road. Leaving debris in their wake. Basically trashing the place."

"And?"

"They want it to stop."

"So they're blocking the road?"

Her father nodded. "They're demanding the convoy turn around."

"But it's got a military escort."

"That's why I'm nervous."

Mika wrinkled her nose.

Her father leaned closer and lowered his voice to a whisper. "You haven't taken a good look at our escorts, but I have. They're young. Real young. I can't believe any of them have ever seen much action. And this isn't a war or a combat zone. These are fellow Americans. Frustrated, hungry, tired Americans."

"So?" Mika didn't understand.

"These young men aren't trained to maintain law and order. They're trained to fight."

A slow realization spread through Mika like a cancer. "Will they shoot them?"

Her father opened his mouth to respond when a volley of cracks echoed through the pass, bouncing off the collapsed mountainside. *Pop-pop-pop. Pop-pop-pop-pop.*

People in the bus began to scream. The soldiers up front hurried to the door, gesticulating at the driver. He pulled the lever and the door opened. All three rushed out, weapons at the ready.

"Was that gunfire?"

Her father nodded.

"Who?" Mika strained to see out a window. "The guards? Or the people from the woods?"

"I don't know, but that's our cue to leave."

"What?" She turned on her father.

His fingers dug into the muscles of her shoulder. "Get ready. We're going to run."

CHAPTER SEVEN
CLINT

Clint Pulled Mika in front of him and gripped her by the upper arms. He leaned close enough to whisper in her ear. "How fast can you move?"

"I...um..." She trailed off.

He jostled her shoulder. "Mika?"

"S—sorry. What did you ask me?"

Clint forced his voice not to betray his emotions. "Nothing. Just stay with me, okay? I need you to stay with me." His daughter was injured, that much he knew. But how badly? He guessed she'd sugarcoated her real status, attempting to mask her injuries so he wouldn't worry. But he noticed how she slept every possible moment and how she winced as she stretched her arms and legs.

Running was risky—they could end up caught in a cross-fire situation or mistaken for a protester by a National Guardsman. But staying on the bus wasn't an option. Mika already lived through one freak accident on the side of a mountain, the sole survivor in a van crowded with dead bodies. If the protestors knocked the bus over or decided to raid it or the National Guard forced them to move and it all went south, they might not make it off alive.

No, they had to leave. Find some place to hide until the commotion ceased and then reassess. He nudged Mika forward. "Ease into the aisle. I'm going to grab our packs. Work your way around people. Slowly."

Mika did as he'd instructed, standing up and edging around the first group of people all jockeying to catch a glimpse of the action out the opposite windows. He dug down beneath the seats and grabbed their backpacks, slinging one over his back and one over his front.

"What're you doing?" It was Bridget, the nurse who'd been kind to them outside.

Clint lowered his voice and ducked his head so only she could hear. "Leaving."

"Do you really think that's a good idea?" She covered her collarbone with a shaky hand. "I swear those were gunshots earlier."

"It's better than staying here."

Bridget frowned. "Is it?"

He didn't have time for this. His gut told him to get off the bus and Clint wasn't waiting around to prove it right or wrong. A volley of gunfire echoed outside and Bridget spun around. He took the opportunity to push Mika forward.

Three rows ahead, an older woman staggered into the aisle, flowing dress ripped in two places, gray hair matted on top of her head. A purpling bruise spread out across her right cheek, a stark contrast to the wadded up tissue she pressed to her lips.

"Excuse me." Mika attempted to sneak by her. As she reached around to use the next seat back as leverage and pull herself past, the woman grabbed her by the shoulder. Bony fingers dug into Mika's skin and she let out a soft cry of alarm.

"Have you seen my little Ricky? He was here a minute ago. But with all the shouting and the commotion —" She dug her hand deeper into Mika's flesh. "He's gone!"

"Let me go!" Mika cried out and Clint rushed in, grabbing the old woman's slender wrist.

"We don't know any Ricky." He pulled the woman's hand off his daughter.

Mika sagged in relief, rubbing her shoulder where the woman's fingers had latched ahold.

"You have to!" The woman turned on Clint, eyes wild with a combination of fear and something not all-together lucid. "He's my baby boy." She cast her gaze all about, frantically turning her head in every direction. "He was just here a minute ago. We're on the way to Chicago. Going to finally see the Windy City."

Clint reached out his arm and held the woman at bay as he ushered Mika to push on. He smiled like he understood. "That sounds great. I'm sure Ricky's just going to the bathroom. He'll be right back."

The woman's face contorted into a smile, all gums and lips. "Oh, I bet you're right. Silly me." She clung to his arm, grip surprisingly firm.

Clint pushed Mika ahead before scooting past the woman. Wherever she was inside her mind, it wasn't the present. He tugged his arm free. "You have a good trip now, okay?"

She smiled, eyes unfocused. "Oh, we will. I promised Ricky we'd go to Wrigley Field." She leaned closer. "I didn't tell him we might see Hank Aguirre." Her whole face lit like she'd won the lottery. "Ricky's got his card from '67. He's not with the Tigers anymore, but he'll still sign it, right?"

Clint let out a breath. Definitely not in the present. He smiled to play along. "Don't see why not. You have a good trip now."

Another volley of gunfire rang out and the woman shrieked. Clint managed to scoot Mika away before she trapped them again. He hustled her down the aisle, darting past worried people, until they neared the front. The bus driver gave them a once-over as they approached.

Clint jerked his head toward the door. "Can you open up?"

"Are you crazy, man? They're shootin' out there."

"That's why I want out of this sitting duck."

The bus driver shook his head. "I've got orders. Everyone's supposed to stay on board."

"Says who?"

"The National Guard."

"You mean those children with rifles?" Clint pressed on his temple. "You really think they know what they're doing? Against a group of armed civilians?"

The bus diver frowned. "I'm just telling you what I know. I'm not supposed to open the door for any reason."

"Dad?"

"Not now, Mika."

"No, Dad?" Mika swooned in front of him, half falling against his chest and half into the seat beside her. He caught her before she slid to the floor.

He looked up at the bus driver, trying his best to convey his worry. "Look, my daughter isn't well. We can't stay here on this bus. She's got to get off. Just open the door, we'll dart out and you can close it right behind us."

The driver hesitated.

A chorus of shots rang out ahead of the bus and something in Clint snapped. "Let us out!" The muscles and tendons in his neck strained against his skin and he surged forward, ready to force the issue. If the driver wouldn't open the door, he'd do it himself.

"Alright, alright!" The bus driver stammered, shoving a hand up in the air. He reached for a lever with his other hand and released the door. It whooshed open and Clint wasted no time. He tugged the pack off his front and shoved it crossbody over his neck before lifting Mika in his arms. He bundled her down the steps and out the door.

Behind them, a commotion rose as other passengers attempted to flee the bus. He didn't have time to turn around. He hoisted Mika up higher and headed around the back, away from the skirmish unfolding in front.

Stumbling to a stop at the rear, Clint sucked in a deep breath and got his bearings. To his left, the mountainside tumbled toward him, mud and dirt and trees pooling on the pavement. To his right, the pass dipped low, tops of pines jutting up through the valley until the opposite side of the highway rose on support columns on the other side. In front of him, another bus sat idling. Behind it must have been at least one Humvee.

He was taking too long. Every second he waited increased their odds of being swept up in the altercation. He took a step forward. The trees were the only source of cover. He'd have to head there and hope none of the protestors still lurked in the shadows.

With a deep breath, he took off, the weight of his daughter and the backpacks turning a run into a slow lope. He crossed the few feet of asphalt before reaching the concrete barriers. He eased Mika over the side. She wobbled on her two feet, barely able to stand.

"Dad?"

He climbed over and reached for her. "Can you walk?"

"I think so."

"Then let's go." He half dragged, half guided her off the edge of the road and into the ferns and weeds and low-lying scrub covering the sloping hill. They stagger-stepped down the side, feet sliding in the loose dirt and rocks. Mika stumbled and it took all of Clint's strength to dive for her and keep her upright. Only thirty more feet and they would be in the cover of trees.

He hurried her along, but she could barely put one foot in front of the other, each third step a trip or slide. They were too exposed. At this rate, someone would spot them before they ever reached the forest.

A shout rang out behind them. Alarm bells jangled in Clint's brain. Without another word to Mika, he scooped her up in his arms again and tried to increase their pace. But the slope was unforgiving. He managed to stay upright, slip-sliding down the rocky embankment, but it was more luck than anything.

"Hey!" Someone shouted close enough for Clint to make out the word. He refused to turn around. They were going to survive this. He just had to keep going. Hurried footsteps and bits of rock and gravel rolling down the slope sounded behind them.

Clint's heart leapt into his throat. He forced his legs to pump harder, his body to move faster. Ten feet. Five. He ducked into the tree line and snaked behind the closest tree, a slim new-growth cedar.

More shouts echoed on the road. He kept going. Sweat slicked his skin between his shoulder blades and coated his palms. Mika clutched his neck, arms wrapped tight as she bounced and jostled in his arms.

As he stepped around a clump of trees, his heel slipped into a hidden hole in the earth and his knees gave way. He collapsed with Mika in his arms. Her hair unspooled from her messy bun and cascaded over his face, covering it like a curtain.

He heard footsteps, the crack of branches, the rustle of leaves, the sound echoing across the woods, bridging the distance. Clint eased Mika back, drawing them both behind the base of a large Douglas fir.

"Don't move," Clint hissed through clenched teeth. The footsteps edged closer and Clint held his breath.

CHAPTER EIGHT
MIKA

Mika blinked over and over, attempting in vain to bring the world into focus. As soon as the shooting started, her pulse spiked and a rush of adrenaline rocketed through her body. Memories flooded back.

Inside her mind, she was back in the van, careening down the side of the mountain, about to lose everyone around her in a horrific crash. Blackness rimmed her vision and ringing in her ears drowned out everything else. She practically panted out each breath. Broken branches and tree roots and body parts flew past her face as her imagination took over. She couldn't see the forest all around her. Couldn't hear her father calling for her.

Not until he shook her whole body back into the present. "Mika!" Her father whisper-shouted into her ear. "Mika, are you with me?"

The thick, heady smell of pine surrounded her and Mika dug her fingers into fresh overturned earth. They were back in a forest, but it wasn't the one she'd barely escaped from. This was new. Maybe even more dangerous. She reached out her dirty fingers and gave her dad's knee a squeeze. She was here. She was alive.

Her father clutched her tight, his thick arms wrapped around her torso as they attempted to disappear behind the bark. "If we're spotted, we have to run. Can you do that?"

Mika nodded, head bumping against the tree bark as she inched into a smaller ball. This wasn't the Girl Scout trip. She'd survived that. Now she was with her father. He would keep her safe.

Branches broke somewhere up the hill, closer than before. Her father tensed. "Ready?"

"Yes." She reached back out, palming the dirt to give her leverage to stand. They both eased up, her dad still holding her by the shoulders, not trusting her strength. She wobbled as her legs extended, but she didn't fall.

After a moment, he let her go. "Stay close." His breath came hot on her cheek. "Follow me."

Her dad's lips turned down in concentration, but his eyes were bright and searching. He was worried.

She tried to smile, give him a bit of encouragement, but whatever she managed to do with her face, it wasn't confidence-inspiring. Her dad's frown slipped into a grimace. They took a few halting steps, attempting to navigate the dense underbrush as quietly as possible.

Something crackled beneath Mika's right boot. Her father swore under his breath.

"Stop! Stop right there!"

Mika turned in slow motion. A figure emerged from

the trees dressed in green camouflage. His tan boots stood out against the dark, loamy earth. But the rifle pointed straight at Mika drew her attention. She stole a sideways glance at her father. He clutched her by the elbow, holding her upright, his grip firm and unyielding.

"Identify yourselves." The soldier waved the rifle at them each in turn, the barrel bobbing a few inches in either direction.

"My name's Clint. This is my daughter, Mika. We're unarmed."

The soldier's Adam's apple bobbed. Mika tried to focus on his face instead of the gun. He didn't look much older than her, maybe a year or two out of high school at most. Pimples pocked his cheeks and razor burn marred his neck. She squinted to read the name tape on his chest. Torres? Tomas? Tower? She couldn't make it out.

"Why did you attack the convoy?"

"Whoa, there." Clint raised his free hand. "You've got the wrong idea. We're from the bus. We were just trying to get to the FEMA shelter when all hell broke loose."

"Not possible."

"Do we look like we're part of some ambush?" Her dad motioned down at the backup clothes he'd bought at Walmart that they'd changed into after swimming through the dirty flood water. "We're exhausted, hungry, barely able to stand and you think *we* attacked *you*?"

The kid frowned as he looked them over. "Orders were to keep the buses secure. No one was allowed off."

"We were." Her dad glanced her way. "My daughter's not well and she's already survived a horrific crash only days ago. I couldn't put her through that again."

"Who said anything about a crash?"

"All I'm saying is that she's been through enough. We had to get off. Take our chances out here."

The rifle bobbed again. "Orders are orders. If you're really from a bus, then you need to head back, now."

Behind them, another volley of gunfire erupted. Mika audibly gasped.

"Listen to it up there," her father protested. "I'm not putting my daughter in the line of fire. It's a death trap."

The kid's eyes narrowed as he gave Mika a long, hard look. "You don't even look related. How do I know you haven't just stolen those packs and this girl and are trying to get away?"

Mika spoke up. "He's my dad. I swear."

"Then tell him he needs to do what's right." He jerked his head toward the hill. "You've got to come with me. Now."

Her father loosened his grip on her elbow to hold out both hands. "Be reasonable here."

"You're the one being unreasonable."

Without her father holding onto her, Mika struggled to stand still. She was all wobbles and fear, adrenaline mixing with her injuries and turning her mind into a tangled mass of flight or fight. The soldier took a step toward them. She recoiled, foot stepping back into a mass of dead branches and scrub.

The rifle jerked in her direction.

Her father held his arms out, as if he could ward off a stray bullet with just his hands.

Mika lost her balance in slow motion, arms windmilling as she landed in a thicket of ferns and brambles. She cried out as her hip contacted the ground. The soldier advanced, rifle pointed straight at her as she lay sprawled out amidst the undergrowth.

The backpacks landed on the ground beside her, one after the other, as her father shed the weight. He turned to her, about to bend down to help her up, when the soldier shouted.

"You! Don't move!" He stared her father down.

After a long moment, her dad eased up, both hands palms out in front of his chest.

The soldier turned back to Mika. "Get up!" He shouted at her, barrel of the gun so close she couldn't focus on anything else. Fear popped her eyelids wide and her pupils dilated, the world all of a sudden too bright and terrifying.

"Get away from my daughter." The words came out guttural and mean and Mika stared up in shock, mouth hanging open. Her father never spoke like that.

The kid ignored the obvious threat and nudged the barrel in Mika's direction. "Get up or I'll shoot."

As soon as the last word left his lips, the hulking shape of her father launched forward, two hundred pounds of overprotective parent careening at a kid half his age. The sound of a shot rang out as the soldier's finger wrapped tight around the trigger. Mika flinched, but the shot went high and wide as the tangle of bodies slammed into the ground.

Feet kicked, arms propelled. One of the men shouted out in pain. Was it her dad? The soldier? Mika had no idea. She crawled backward on her palms like a crab, putting distance between her and the ground fight.

At last, her father rose on his knees, both hands clutching the rifle still attached to the kid by a strap around his torso. Her father brought the butt of the gun up and down with wicked force, slamming it into the side of the kid's head. All of a sudden it was over.

Her father leaned back on his heels and sucked in a violent breath. Sweat coated his brow and face. His body shook. Mika swallowed hard and turned to the soldier, now unconscious on the ground.

She ran her tongue over dry lips. "Did you—?"

Her father reached for the kid's neck, feeling for a pulse. "He's still alive."

Mika closed her eyes in relief.

"We need to move."

"But—"

She opened her eyes to find her father already standing, one backpack on his back, the other in his hands. He positioned the second one on his chest before easing down to slide the rifle strap off the unconscious soldier. He hoisted the gun up and draped the strap over his shoulder. "Ready?"

Mika was still woozy, but no longer so afraid. She forced the butterflies swarming in her chest to slow. "Are we just going to leave him here?"

Her father stared down at the unconscious lump blending into the surrounding leaves. "Yep."

"But—"

"He could have killed you, sweetheart."

"But—"

"We can't be here when someone else comes looking." He held out his free hand. "Let's go."

She reached up and let her father haul her up. It didn't seem right to leave the kid there, unconscious on the ground. But her father was right. He didn't believe them when they explained where they came from. If more National Guardsmen found them like this, with a soldier on the ground, they might shoot first and never ask a single question.

"Which way?" She glanced around her, unsure where they were, let alone which direction to go.

Her father nodded straight ahead. "Down this ravine and into the valley. We'll need to skirt around whatever is happening out there."

"Won't we be heading straight into it?"

"Not if we give a wide enough berth. We'll head for the overpass with I-90 running in the opposite direction and track it toward Ellensburg. As long as we keep it in our sights, we'll be headed the right way."

Mika hesitated. "Are you sure we shouldn't go back to the buses?"

Her dad ran a hand over the back of his neck. "No. I'm not. But I think it's too late to go back. We'll be caught in the crossfire or worse."

The ravine continued down below them, cedars and

fir trees clinging to the hillside, eventually blending into a sea of green some distance below. Mika couldn't gauge how far they needed to travel to reach the other segment of the highway. But it wasn't close. With a deep breath, she picked up first one foot and then the other. It would be slow going, but she would try. The sooner they left this mountain pass behind, the sooner they would find her mom.

CHAPTER NINE
DAPHNE

A plume of dust billowed out behind them as the truck bounced along the old logging road. Dirt crunched under the tires. Bits of rock clinked against the bottom frame. Daphne stared out the windshield, lost in quiet introspection. Jocelyn lightly snored beside her.

Samuel twisted in the driver's seat and gave her a smile. "Sorry, there's not much to look at on these back roads."

Daphne managed to smile and readjusted herself in the seat. She wedged her hands between her thighs. "It's fine. More than fine, actually."

There was nothing but wilderness on either side of the road, a dense plot of woods hugging close to either side, threatening to invade it. No houses. No cars. No buildings. No visible touch of man other than the remains of the road. Judging by the weeds growing up through the dirt, it hadn't been traveled by a vehicle in a long time. She was grateful it wasn't winter when the entire area would be blanketed in impassable snow.

For once since this whole catastrophic unfolding of events happened, Daphne had a flicker of hope that maybe they were going to make it out of this in one piece. "I can't believe we're finally out of the city."

Samuel yawned and stretched his neck back and forth. "If I never see water or the ocean again, I'll be a happy man."

Daphne laughed. "You don't mean that, but I get it."

"Nothing's going to be the same in the Pacific Northwest, that's for sure."

"Not for a good long while, at least," Daphne agreed, staring for a long moment at Samuel's profile. Here she was, driving along a dirt road in the middle of nowhere with a strange man she didn't really know, covered in dirt and stink. And yet she was almost happy. Life threw crazy curve balls.

Jocelyn stirred beside Daphne, smacked her lips, and sighed.

"At least one of us is getting some beauty sleep."

Samuel chuckled. "She's recharging that feisty spirit."

Daphne laughed, and it felt good. "She sure is."

"What are you going to do after this?" Samuel tilted his head toward Daphne. "Are you ever going back to the metro?"

She shook her head. There was nothing left for her there anymore. All she wanted now was to reunite with her family.

"It's probably for the best. I've heard Portland's more or less the same. Everyone will have to start over, rebuild."

"I'm not sure I want to be a part of all that." Daphne glanced at him. "What about you? What are your plans?"

"To be honest, I'm not sure. I'll probably just take it day by day for a while. My daughter lives in Montana. I might go there."

She nodded in agreement.

"I used to live in a logging camp, back when I was real young," Samuel shared. "The story I'm going to tell you is going to date me, and yes, I really am *that* old." He paused and his eyes twinkled.

Daphne warmed. It felt like forever since she'd been this comfortable. This calm for longer than a moment. "You're in luck, because I love a good story."

"I've lived around here my whole life. As soon as I was old enough to get a job, I chose the logging life." He paused again, pensive. "Or maybe it chose me."

She nodded, listening.

"We'd cleared a rail line connecting a large timber property to a mill. Once the line went in, we had to log it all. Thousands of acres. To save time, we created a little shanty town right on the edge of the line."

He smiled at the memory. "Basically a spit of cleared ground where we set up tents and lived while we worked the job. By the time I'd been working there a while, the project grew, and so did our crew. Toward the end of the job, we had almost fifty men working, all pulling their own weight, with their own responsibilities. All young guys like me who could lift heavy equipment and were in good physical shape." He patted his hip and shook his head. "Not so much in shape anymore, I'm afraid."

She smiled and waited for him to continue.

"There was this real sense of community, you know? All of us in this common, shared pursuit, all working for the same thing. But then the project finished and the land was logged and we all moved on." He glanced down at the steering wheel and his old, weathered hands. "Everyone moved on to different jobs, different lives. I never saw any of them again."

Daphne gave a start. It wasn't the story she'd expected him to tell. "Why not? Why didn't you keep in touch?"

Samuel's shoulders hitched in an unflappable shrug. "That was the way of it back then. Things came and went, but some things stayed the same."

"Like?"

"Me, for one. I am who I am. Doesn't matter if I'm hauling towering pines off to a mill or driving a pretty young lady halfway across the state."

She smiled down at her hands. "I'm not that young, Samuel."

"It's all relative, I suppose." He hitched himself higher in the seat. "What I'm tryin' to say is that everyone who survived this is now suffering in Seattle, and Portland, and all the little towns in between. But the people of the Pacific Northwest are resilient. We're strong and we can conquer any challenge. Material things can be rebuilt. After all, we're still standing, aren't we?"

Daphne thought about it for a long moment. Sure, Samuel was able to move on and rebuild when he was a young man, but that had to be what, forty years ago? People were different now. She opened her mouth to try to put it into words when the truck sputtered, jostling them.

Samuel looked baffled. "What the heck?" He leaned over the dash.

"What's wrong?" Daphne's heart jumped into her throat.

The truck sputtered again. The engine made a sighing sound, hissed, and stalled out. The quietness blanketed them.

"Out of gas." Samuel thumped a fist against the steering wheel.

Daphne's muscles froze. "Out of gas? How can that be? We checked it in the parking garage and there was plenty."

Samuel reached for the driver's door and wrenched it open. It whined in protest. "That's what the dash says."

He hopped out of the car and walked around to the side, where the gas tank was located. A loud curse sounded from the rear and something thumped against the side.

Jocelyn startled awake. "What's going on?" Her voice was raspy with sleep.

Samuel returned and motioned to the back of the

truck. "Darn thing's got a leak. Looks like the gas tank was cracked in the crash that caused the gash down the side."

"Then why wasn't it already empty when we found it? We didn't smell any gas in the parking deck."

Samuel frowned. "I'm guessing when I drove over the curb and the back end slammed down, it cracked more—enough to leak. It must have been leaking ever since."

Daphne blew out a breath of frustration. "What are we going to do now?"

Samuel scratched the top of his head. "We're going to have to walk, I suppose."

"*Walk?*" Jocelyn groaned.

Samuel shrugged. "I don't know that we have a choice. We're lucky we got this far."

"We're stranded in the middle of nowhere." Jocelyn shoved her head between her knees.

Daphne rubbed her back. "Just try to calm down. We need to save our energy."

Jocelyn eyed her. "Did I tell you I'm not much of a nature gal?" She sucked in a breath and hoisted the door open. "I need to see this leak for myself."

Daphne followed and together they walked around to the rear of the truck. Samuel bent and motioned toward the undercarriage. Daphne crouched down. Jocelyn hemmed and hawed for a long moment, but eventually kneeled on the ground to catch a glimpse. Sure enough, the remains of the truck's gas etched a wet line down a portion of rusted metal.

Jocelyn cursed beneath her breath and struggled to

stand. "We left all the crazy behind, but now we're out here in the wilderness with nothing. Maybe we should have just waited and gotten on another bus. Taken our chances. At least we would have eventually made it to a shelter."

"Not necessarily," Samuel countered. "It's not like it's going to get any better out there. At least here we're on our own."

"Yeah, without food or water or shelter. I don't know about you, but these sandals ain't made for walkin'."

Daphne almost laughed even though it wasn't the least bit funny. "At least you have shoes."

Samuel cracked a smile. "Look, I'm not as agile as I used to be, but I know the back roads, and eventually we'll hit a paved one."

Daphne clamped a supportive hand over Jocelyn's shoulder. "We're going to have to do our best for now."

"I'm tired of being strong."

Daphne patted her shoulder. "Me too. We all are."

She stole a glance at Samuel. He was wincing as he hobbled around the side of the truck. Her heart and her mind fused with worry. He was too old to hike for who knew how many miles and Jocelyn was on the verge of a meltdown.

But what other choice did they have? After a few moments to regroup, they set off, walking in the direction the truck had been headed, three abreast on the dirt road. Daphne tried to keep everyone's spirits up, asking questions about their lives before everything fell apart.

At first, it worked, but after an hour, they lapsed into uncomfortable, exhausted silence. Jocelyn fretted and moaned beside her and Samuel practically limped with each step. If they didn't find a road soon, they would need to rest for the night.

Daphne slipped into her own world of jumbled thoughts. She worried about her daughter and Clint, wondered if they were still at the shelter in Ellensburg or if they'd already moved on when they discovered she wasn't there. Maybe Jocelyn was right; they should have gotten on another bus. But she couldn't bear it.

The same seats, same dark-tinted windows. Same risk of an ambush or a crash. No, even though this might take longer, it was better. They would reach civilization and find another way to the main shelter. She was sure of it.

"Guys?"

Daphne lifted her head.

Jocelyn pointed. "Is that—?"

Daphne squinted against the dimming light of early evening. While they'd been hiking, clouds had crowded the horizon, low hanging and heavy with unshed rain. She blinked. Was the light playing tricks on her, showing her things that weren't there? She rubbed her right eye. No, it was real. What appeared to be the outline of a small house separated from the trees. She smiled in relief. "See? I knew we'd find civilization."

"Don't say it till we actually make it," Jocelyn warned.

Daphne shook off the other woman's doubt and

reached for her hand, squeezing tight. With a smile at Samuel, they stayed the course together, finally about to be out of the woods and somewhere they could regroup and rest.

CHAPTER TEN
CLINT

Clint inhaled the rich scent of damp earth and pine, bringing back countless memories of the hiking and camping trips he'd taken with Mika throughout the years. But now, the weight of responsibility for his injured daughter added a heaviness to which no backpack could compare. Each time he glanced at Mika, her youth and vulnerability were stark reminders of the stakes.

She'd almost died on a mountain so similar less than a week ago. Then again in the flood water. The soldier back there, barely old enough to vote, almost shot her point blank. Visions of her bleeding out twisted his insides and he swallowed down a rising wave of acid in his throat. It was his job to protect her, to keep her safe, and he felt like he'd almost failed over and over.

Maybe she was right; maybe they would have been better off staying on the bus and taking their chances. But his gut told him to leave, that they would be safer on their own.

As they slowly descended the hill, the ground beneath his boots shifted unpredictably. Bits of gravel rolled and slid underfoot and branches crunched beneath his weight. A patch of moss slicked his boot and he slid across a sloped bit of exposed rock, arms windmilling as he almost fell.

"Watch out for that one." He pointed at the slippery strip of green and Mika nodded, stepping wide.

He reached out as they navigated through a tight spot between two trees and his knuckles grazed the rough texture of the bark. Another few steps and a breeze rustled the trees, but it brought no familiar sounds. No birds chirping, no animals roving about in the underbrush. The firefight up above put an end to all that. Beside him, Mika slipped and cried out, but he caught her, fingers clutching at her forearm as she steadied herself.

Each step they took was a testament to his determination. Guided by instincts honed over the years, he navigated the descent, always ensuring that Mika was within arm's reach. While he was accustomed to the unpredictability of nature, he couldn't help but be hyper-aware of every potential danger. With each careful step, he aimed to shield his daughter from the harsher realities of their circumstance.

She was mirroring his movements, picking her steps carefully, her fingers occasionally brushing the tips of ferns that lined their path. The afternoon sun cast elongated shadows across the uneven terrain, hiding dangers from their view. Mika took a step and suddenly her whole body twisted. A gnarled root, hidden beneath a bed of fallen pine needles, threw her entire body out of balance.

"Mika!" Clint called out as he reached for her, but he wasn't fast enough.

Time seemed to slow as he watched, heart in his throat, Mika tumbling down the incline. Branches snapped and leaves rustled violently in the fleeting chaos. She landed with a sharp gasp, her body jolting as it met the ground. For a heartbeat, everything was eerily silent except for the echo of the fall reverberating through the woods and the pounding of his own heart.

Rushing to her side, he noticed the reddening skin on her forearm where she'd tried to brace her fall and the grimace of pain on her face. His hands trembled slightly as he reached out to her, brushing away the debris and leaves clinging to her clothes. "Talk to me, Mika," he urged, trying to keep his voice steady and mask the undercurrent of fear threatening to break through.

"I... I think I'm okay, Dad," she replied, her voice shaky and punctuated with sharp intakes of breath. As he gently probed the scraped forearm, she winced. The raw wound looked superficial, but it was clearly painful.

"Where else does it hurt?" he asked, maintaining eye contact to read any unspoken distress.

A single tear slipped down Mika's cheek and she rubbed it away with the palm of her hand. "Nowhere."

"Are you sure?"

She nodded and wiped at her face again, scrubbing her cheeks until they colored from the effort. "I'm okay."

She snuffed back a rush of snot in her nose and tried to calm, but he could see the strain. She was close to falling apart. Close to melting down right there, too close to the firefight to be safe. They needed to press on.

Clint reached out and gave her uninjured arm a squeeze. "Hey, it's okay. Injuries happen. You were hurt before we even started this hike." Clint smiled at her with a mix of apology and sympathy. "Maybe we should have stayed on the bus."

"What about the shoot out?"

He shrugged. "Maybe they would have given up."

"Dad." She pinned him with a teenage stare. "Don't be ridiculous. You said this was the best way out of here and it still is. Stop trying to make me feel better."

"It isn't working?"

Mika managed to smile through her tears. "Not even close."

Clint leaned back and rested his palms on his thighs. At least he'd pulled her out of the funk. "So what do we do now?"

"Exactly what you said before. We keep going."

"And if you can't?"

"Then we regroup and figure out a new plan."

He smiled, a genuine one brimming with love. "Love you, kiddo."

"Love you, too, Dad."

Mika reached to pull her sleeve down, but winced when the fabric touched her arm. "You wouldn't by any chance have any pain meds would you?"

"Nope." He scrunched up one cheek. "That bad,

huh?"

"It's like a rug burn. Hurts whenever I touch it."

"Then let's try to avoid that, shall we?"

Mika reached out and grabbed the closest thing—a clump of pine needles clinging to a nearby branch—and tossed it at him.

"Hey! What was that for?"

"Teasing." She almost laughed. "Now let's get down this stupid ravine so we can find some place that isn't full of angry people with guns, okay?"

Clint breathed out in relief and picked up the packs and rifle. Together, they headed further down the mountain, slower than before, but still making progress. The sun lowered in the sky, a crimson orb dipping below the tree line as they hiked.

They both fell silent, Mika concentrating on the placement of her feet, Clint on any sign his daughter might fall again. As the sun dipped lower, Clint fought the urge to speed up. Every few steps, he glanced around them, searching for a suitable place to rest and make camp.

They didn't have many supplies, certainly nothing to create a shelter out of, but there were fallen branches here and there. If he could pull down a few still lush with needles, they might be able to fashion a small lean-to and shelter from the cold overnight. His thoughts drifted to the necessary preparations and he forgot about the altercation back on the road.

"Do you remember that overnight trip we took to Juniper Dunes? You must have been eight, maybe nine?"

Mika glanced toward the sky, thinking. "The one where mom almost stepped on the skunk?"

Clint chuckled. "The one and only. We'd been hiking from the parking area to the designated wilderness on that rutted OHV trail, remember?"

Mika nodded. "It was almost like a sand rollercoaster, all these mounds and hills one after the other."

"That's right. And then we rounded that clump of scrub brush and your mom screamed."

Mika giggled. "That skunk had been minding its own business, perfectly happy munching on some giant bug it'd managed to catch and then there was Mom, almost stepping on its tail!"

"I've never seen your mother jump so fast in her life."

"Not fast enough, though. Didn't she have to throw those boots away?"

Clint laughed again at the memory. "She tried everything—baking soda, dish soap, even soaking them in tomato juice. Nothing worked. Even her feet smelled for a few days."

Mika joined in the laughter, both of their spirits buoyed by the memory. "I think that was the last time mom went camping with us voluntarily."

"You might be right about that. Definitely the last time we went to the dunes."

"But it was so pretty. I'm glad we went back later. It was fun to do that hike. Especially in the spring when all the flowers bloom. You'd never think a desert area would have so much plant life."

Clint nodded. The packs were still heavy across his

shoulders, but seeing and hearing his daughter come alive while reminiscing about the past lifted some of the hidden weight. They'd been mired in doom and gloom and the potential horrors of their situation for so long, it felt good to think about something joyful. Something positive.

They would get there again. They just had to keep going. Find a way out of this ravine and into Ellensburg and on to Daphne. Once they found her, there were so many things he wanted to say. So many missed opportunities to rekindle what they'd once had.

Maybe they would regroup. Find some common ground.

His thoughts drifted to all the good times they had over the years. All the circumstances that brought them joy. It was always the little moments, sometimes mundane like the day he realized Mika stopped asking for help tying her shoes, and sometimes monumental, like the first time she drove away, a sixteen-year-old with a driver's license, all on her own.

He wanted more of those memories to include Daphne. Mika would be leaving soon. She would go off to college and a new life that didn't revolve around their little family unit. He wanted Daphne by his side when it happened. He wanted his wife back.

Clint began to formulate a plan in his mind, what he'd say to her when he saw her again after all this time. After all they'd each been through.

A fresh volley of gunfire brought him screaming back into the present.

CHAPTER ELEVEN
CLINT

The shape of the ravine made it impossible to judge the distance or direction of the gunfire with any precision. But Clint pulled Mika into a crouch behind a large Red Cedar and pressed a finger to his lips all the same. They waited like that, both snugged low and tight against the fragrant bark, until he was sure they were safe to proceed.

"All right," he whispered. "Let's keep going, but stay close and ears open."

Mika nodded.

The guardsman's rifle gave Clint a bit of confidence he'd lacked up until now. They weren't entirely defenseless, despite the lack of law and order. He didn't want to shoot anyone, but he would if he had to. To protect his daughter. To protect himself.

Clint stared up at the sky. They were an hour or more from sunset, but the cloud cover turned the forest dark, elongating shadows and distorting their vision. He squinted into the trees, searching for some semblance of a path.

He dug into his pack and pulled out his hooded sweatshirt. "If it rains, hopefully it isn't heavy."

After a moment, they resumed their trek. Eventually, the terrain leveled and they found themselves following a well-worn animal trail across the forest floor. The first raindrops pattered the pine needles and Clint pulled up his hood.

Maybe they should have sought out shelter already, but he'd hoped to be further from the busses before they made camp. He picked up the pace, encouraging Mika to hike a bit faster on the even ground. The trail wove through the trees mostly parallel with the highway above.

They made good time and thanks to the dense tree canopy, stayed mostly dry as the rain continued to lightly fall. After about an hour, as the sun slipped below the trees and sunset shrouded the forest in darkness, Clint called out for Mika to stop.

Based on his best estimates, they were a mile or two from the buses. While he'd have loved to be ten times that distance away, they hadn't heard a shout or a round of gunfire after the last burst. They were as safe as they were going to be and they needed to hunker down for the night.

They made camp in a little den of close-set cedar trees, their branches overlapping above and providing a modicum of shelter. It wasn't much, but it was better than nothing. Mika snuggled down beside him, curling into a tight ball, head on his shoulder.

Clint stared out into the encroaching darkness.

"Aren't you going to sleep?"

He smiled down at his daughter. Although he could no longer see her face, he heard the concern in her voice. He patted her knee. "Don't worry about me. You get some rest. We'll set off first thing in the morning."

Mika mumbled another weak protest, but she fell asleep within moments, the terror and exhaustion of the day overwhelming her body. Clint sat motionless, hand resting on the rifle. He would stay awake as long as he could, watching. Things would improve in the morning. He had to remain positive.

Clint awoke with a start. His fingers twitched against the rifle as he remembered where he was. Mika shifted slightly beside him, her head now resting squarely on his chest. The first hints of daylight filtered through the trees and humid air, coating everything in a thin layer of mist and damp.

Straight ahead, no more than fifteen feet, a buck with velvet-covered antlers stood stock still, appraising him. From the sheer size of him, Clint guessed mule deer, but he wasn't a hundred percent thanks to the dimness of the morning light. They watched each other, neither moving for an extended moment. The buck blew out a short breath and it clouded in the humid air.

Despite everything that happened the week before, the quake and the tsunami, and the total destruction of both natural coastline and man-made cities, nature continued its steady rhythm. After a long moment, the buck took one step. A pause. Another step. When Clint made no movement, the animal finally approached, cleaving to the worn and beaten path ten feet to his right.

Clint watched him pass, holding his breath until the animal slipped out of sight. As he shifted position at last, Mika woke, groaning as she sat up and rubbed the sleep marks etched across her cheek.

"What time is it?"

"I'm guessing early morning. Maybe seven. How'd you sleep?"

"Like I was caught out in the rain all night." She stretched and reached for her pack. "We still have a bit of food, right?"

"I think there's a few granola bars left."

Mika dug in the pack and they made a quick breakfast of the last of their provisions from Clint's rushed expedition to Walmart. It had only been a few days, but it felt like a lifetime ago. They packed quickly and set off, continuing to follow the deer trail through the forest. As they walked, the trail angled toward the road, edging up a shallower grade of the mountainside than they'd climbed down the day before.

"Don't we want to stay in the valley?" Mika asked as they climbed.

Clint shook his head. "No. Eventually we need the road. I think we're far enough from where we stopped last night that it'll be safe. We'll just follow this trail and if it turns back toward the valley, we'll cut through the forest until we reach the asphalt."

Mika nodded and turned back to the trail,

concentrating to place her feet securely on the damp earth. They were both a bit damp, Clint more than Mika, but if they reached the road, he hoped a day of sunshine would dry their clothes. At least his feet were dry and the air around them warmed with every notch of the sun higher in the sky.

After another hour of concerted, steady effort, they reached the road.

"Dad?"

"Mm-hmm?" Clint asked while not looking up. He pulled his sweatshirt off and draped it over the backpack on his back in hopes it would dry. "What is it?"

"Isn't that our bus?"

He jerked his head up in an instant and squinted into the glare of the morning sun, now bright above the tree line. Sure enough, a FEMA bus with its familiar white and blue paint lay sprawled across the pavement, tipped over on its side about two hundred feet ahead. Clint swallowed and reached for his daughter. "Stay behind me."

She followed his instructions, waiting for him to load the backpacks back onto his back and front before creeping forward. Clint gripped the rifle in both hands as he climbed the last three feet onto the shoulder. He scanned the road for any sign of movement. He found none. After motioning for Mika to follow, they both advanced on the bus, heads on swivels searching for any sign of life.

A body lay sprawled across the pavement. Followed by another and another. Mika sucked in a breath beside him. The familiar cut and color of a nurse's uniform stood out against the pavement. *Bridget*. the woman who'd helped Mika when she'd fainted at the picnic table. Past her, the old woman with the torn dress and the loose grip on reality lay face down, neck twisted at an impossible angle.

This was their bus. Clint reached for Mika's hand. If they'd stayed on it and waited out the ambush, they might be dead now. Together, they approached the vehicle, Clint listening for any sign of life. "We need to check the bus. See if anyone's still alive."

Mika clutched his arm. "Where's the National Guard? Shouldn't they be here?"

"Maybe this bus got left behind. Or maybe they were already here, searching for survivors and are dropping them off at the shelter before coming back for the bodies. Maybe—"

"They're all dead."

Clint shook his head. "Not possible."

Mika pressed her lips into a line and said no more. Clint patted her hand as they continued to walk, clearing the corner of the bus to head toward the front. They would have to climb on top to reach the door, but it would be worth it. If even one person was alive inside...

The rumble of an engine caught Clint off-guard and he grabbed Mika. They pressed tight against the bus, trying to squeeze behind a tire. From his vantage point, Clint could make out a slice of road. A red Toyota Tacoma on a lift kit squealed to a stop beside the bus and a young man threw open the driver's side door.

"Yo! Jimmy! You still in there?" The man was young, maybe twenty-two or three, with spiky brown hair and a know-it-all grin. He slapped the roof of the truck as he hollered again. "Yo! Jimmy!"

"Don't get your panties in a twist, I'm comin'." Another man's voice came from the bus and Mika shuddered beside him. Clint closed his eyes for a brief moment. There was someone alive inside the bus, but it wasn't a crash survivor. If they'd been a few minutes faster, Clint would have come face to face with the guy as soon as he'd jumped down through the open bus door.

The bus vibrated as the other man climbed over the edge and landed on the ground on the other side, near the roof. Clint exhaled in relief. He held Mika tight as the man strolled toward the idling Tacoma.

"You'll never believe the haul outta this thing, man. Two iPads, like eight phones, and a laptop. Who knew people cared more about their electronics than clothes, right?"

"I did." The guy with the truck slapped the roof again. "Come on, man. We're already late. Mick won't give us a good price if we're not the first ones there."

"All right, all right."

Clint watched with a caught breath as both men piled into the truck and drove off, back in the direction they'd come. After a handful of minutes, he finally released Mika and they sagged to the ground.

"That was close."

"Too close."

"Were they stealing?"

Clint nodded.

"From dead people?"

"Seems so."

Mika shuddered. "If we'd stayed on the bus—"

"I know." Clint pushed up to stand. "Let's get out of here before someone else comes looking."

He waited for his daughter to place her hand in his before pulling her gently up. Together, they hurried past the bus and resumed their trek toward Ellensburg. Clint held the rifle at the ready. He wouldn't be caught off-guard like that again.

CHAPTER TWELVE
DAPHNE

"What *is* this place?" Jocelyn's eyes widened and her pupils dilated as she squinted into the dark, black shrinking the copper brown of her irises to a thin ring.

What Daphne had originally taken for a tiny town rising out of the overgrown weeds was nothing more than a smattering of abandoned houses. Moss and lichen grew on the wood shingles and dark holes gaped and mawed where windows used to be.

Samuel scratched at a spot behind his ear. "It's been a long time, but I remember this place."

"You *do*?" Jocelyn's voice pitched higher. Her face twisted into a disgusted grimace as she peered at the closest building, a little shed with thin boards nailed over the windows, each one covered in flecks of peeling paint.

Samuel chuckled and rubbed his hand over his beard. "Used to be a logging town. A more robust version of the place I was telling Daphne about while you were sleeping."

"What happened to it?"

"A bunch of fires ripped through the area about a hundred years ago so the logging all dried up."

Daphne shook her head. "These houses can't have been vacant that long. They'd have all fallen down by now."

"Oh, people lived here for a lot longer. I went to school with a kid whose grandma refused to move. She wasn't the only one, though." Samuel paused for a moment while he took stock. "Back in the 80s, there were probably five or ten houses still occupied. But without any real jobs out here in the wilderness, most people moved on by the 1950s, I think."

Daphne walked over to a small house with two busted windows and a missing front door. She stepped onto the collapsing front porch, avoiding a massive, rotten hole. "There's a sign stuck on here." She rubbed at it with the heel of her palm. "City of Tacoma. Notice of Condemnation." She rubbed a bit harder. "Looks like it was put on in the early 2000s."

She ducked her head inside the door.

"That can't be safe," Jocelyn called out. "It's been condemned."

"There's still stuff in here. An old white metal stove, A fridge." She swallowed. "There's dishes on the table. Bowls and cups. It's like someone just got up one day and walked out after breakfast. Never came back."

"Maybe they did."

"Okay, now you both are giving me the creeps." Jocelyn rubbed her upper arms to ward off an imaginary chill. "I don't think we should be poking around in this place. What if someone's still living here?"

"Unlikely."

"You said there are dishes."

"With about an inch of dust on top. And I don't see any footprints on the floor. Just a bunch of trash and maybe some animal nests."

Jocelyn made a noise and backed away.

Daphne understood the other woman's reluctance, but it was late. Within the hour, the entire forest would descend into darkness. They needed to find shelter. Fast. "It's sunset. We need to stop for the night."

"Here? No." Jocelyn crossed her hands back and forth in front of her. "No way."

A fat raindrop landed on Daphne's forehead and she again flicked her eyes up to the sky. "Do you want to be caught out in the weather instead?"

Jocelyn groaned.

While they'd been talking, Samuel had trekked on ahead, poking his head in open windows, and peering into the dark, abandoned spaces of the few buildings still standing.

"This one has promise," Samuel called out from about forty feet down the overgrown road.

Daphne ushered Jocelyn to follow and together they dodged clumps of weeds and bushes growing through the remains of a gravel drive to find Samuel on the porch of what appeared to be a more or less intact structure. Without waiting for the women, Samuel tried the door. It yielded, creaking as it opened.

Jocelyn reached for Daphne's hand and together they waited as Samuel ducked inside the building. The darkening sky barely illuminated the inside of the building and Samuel's shape blended into the interior. But after a moment, something began to glow.

Daphne stepped forward, pulling Jocelyn with her. A lighter lit Samuel's face with an orange glow as he reappeared in the entryway. "Looks like this place was set up for tours. I'm guessing someone made a bit of cash telling spooky stories about the town, guided ghost tours, that sort of thing."

"But it's abandoned?"

"Looks that way. Maybe only in the last couple of years."

"So it's clean?" The hope in Jocelyn's voice made Daphne smile.

Samuel gave a satisfactory nod. "Mostly."

Daphne pulled Jocelyn again toward the building. "Come on, it's the best option." She glanced again at the sky. "I don't think we have long before the rain starts coming down."

Samuel backed up and the women stepped inside the little house. Shadows danced across the floors and walls, playing tricks on Daphne's brain.

"Smells dusty in here." Jocelyn wrapped her arms around herself and stood stock still in the middle of the room.

"Looks like it's been shut up for quite a while," Daphne offered. "At least the windows are intact."

"Door, too." Samuel walked toward the rear of the

single room and what appeared to be a business counter of sorts. He ducked behind it and the entire place dipped into darkness as he bent with the lighter.

Jocelyn sucked in an audible breath.

Daphne attempted to stay calm. There was nothing to be afraid of inside the place. They were just in the dark.

After a long moment of Samuel rustling around beneath the counter, he stood up in a rush. The flame on his lighter guttered. "Daphne, can you hold this?"

He thrust something in her direction and she stepped forward. A candle. Her shoulders slumped in relief. "Of course." She held the base of the white wax while Samuel lit the wick.

"There's a box of emergency candles down here. Four or five still in there. We just need something to shove it in to stand up."

Daphne held the candle aloft while Samuel searched.

"This'll work." He dumped the dusty contents of a little dish on the counter and took the candle from Daphne's outstretched hand. He used his lighter to melt a bit of the bottom and then shoved it onto the dish, holding it steady until the wax hardened before setting it on the counter. "There we go."

Daphne smiled at Jocelyn, who still stood in the same place in the middle of the room. "It's not so bad now. At least we can see."

"Speak for yourself. I'm not moving until you both tell me I'm not going to step on a rat or a dead body."

Daphne chuckled and came around the side of the counter to help Samuel search. If there were candles, they might find something else useful. She didn't hold out much hope for food, but as soon as Samuel opened the wall cabinets her heart practically leapt. "Is that—?"

"Yep." He reached out and plucked two cans of Spam off the shelf. "Guess these people were prepared for all situations."

Jocelyn made a gagging sound. "Please tell me there's something else in there."

Samuel fished around. "Looks like a four-year-expired box of crackers. I wouldn't touch that if I were you. Probably rancid."

"There must be pretty serious snowfall here in the winter," Daphne guessed. "I wouldn't be surprised if this place was basically cut off for long periods of time."

"There were power lines at one point." Samuel jerked his head toward the front of the building. "Saw the pole out front. No wires now, though."

Daphne dug around beneath the counter, searching for anything else they could use. The patter of rainfall sounded on the metal roof as she rifled through a stack of papers coated in dust. One, a faded flyer with hanging numbers to pull off caught her eye. She pulled it out and held it close to the candle light. A small, four-seater prop plane was showcased in the center. "Snoqualmie Pass aerial tours available daily. Call for price."

She squinted to read the rest. "Snoqualmie Airfield. Two miles due West of Abbeville. Guided hikes available. Ask at tour station." She glanced up. "Are we in Abbeville?"

Samuel thought it over. "Maybe?" He kept searching through the rest of the cabinets as Daphne bent back underneath the counter and pulled out the rest of the papers. It didn't take more than a few minutes to confirm. They were apparently standing in the Abbeville Ghost and Nature Tour Center offering guided day and twilight hikes three days a week.

She tapped her finger on the faded airplane tour flyer. "I..." She trailed off.

"What?" Samuel stopped searching and turned to her.

"I took flying lessons a long time ago."

"You did?" Jocelyn spoke up. While they had been busy searching for any more food or supplies, Jocelyn had managed to collect herself enough to clear off a small table near the window. She sat at one of the chairs, waiting.

A flood of memories swept Daphne in that moment. Climbing into a little prop plane for the first time. Her instructor sitting beside her as she managed to take off unassisted. Flying high over rural Washington state. Meeting Clint.

She smiled at nothing. "It was where I met my husband."

"Clint?"

She nodded. "We'd accidentally been double booked for a lesson. I was going to reschedule, but Clint offered to let me share his slot. We could both fly for half the time. I ended up sitting behind him for his portion of the lesson and, well, we hit it off." She shook her head. "But that was a long time ago."

"Can you still fly?"

Daphne sucked in a breath and held it for a long moment. "I think so."

Jocelyn was pensive as she focused on the table. "Are you sure? I don't want to get a few thousand feet off the ground and have you all of a sudden reconsider."

A laugh slipped past Daphne's lips. "Neither do I." But the more she thought about it, the more her confidence grew. Sure, she'd be rusty. But flying was a lot like driving because of muscle memory. It became almost background noise.

Besides, finding this place, finding the flyer for the airstrip...

She couldn't help but feel it was a sign. Like she was headed in the right direction. Back to her family. Back to everything she loved. She blinked in rapid succession, willing unbidden tears to retreat. Port Angeles might not have been glamorous, or the big city life that she wanted, but it had been home. A place with the two people she loved most in the whole world.

If—*no, when*—she found Clint and Mika, she would make it right.

Daphne inhaled deep and slow and rested her palm on top of the flyer. "It's a long shot, but the airfield's in the right direction. If the place still exists and there's a working plane, I can fly it. I can fly us to Ellensburg."

"Then it sounds like we've got a plan." Samuel

popped open the first can of Spam and held it out. "Who's hungry?"

CHAPTER THIRTEEN
DAPHNE

Daphne's breath came quick as she walked beside Jocelyn. Each step was deliberate, the forest floor crisp and cool beneath her bare feet. Sunlight pierced the dense canopy in sharp, golden beams. A scent of damp moss and pine needles rode the air, a mix of decay and fresh growth. Ahead, a clearing emerged, partially hidden by the remains of a chain link fence. The pair of them hesitated, waiting for Samuel to catch up.

He hadn't mentioned his hip yet, but Daphne sensed it gave him considerable trouble. Between the three of them, he struggled the most, even though Daphne's feet were torn and blistered from the days without shoes.

The three of them stood on the edge of a clearing. An old control tower, skeletal and half-devoured by ivy, loomed in the center. Overgrown grass raced to claim the abandoned airstrip, but nature hadn't finished its takeover. As the sun breached the horizon, it painted the airfield in a fiery blaze. Scarlet and amber light caught on the dew-tipped roof of a small hangar, turning it to molten gold. Birds cried above, their songs juxtaposing against the silent strip of asphalt below.

"It looks just as overgrown as the town." Jocelyn worried her hands as she looked around.

Samuel slipped two fingers into the slots of the fence separating them from the airfield. "Might have to climb this."

"That is *not* happening." Jocelyn crossed her arms.

Daphne pressed her lips into a line. The prospect of climbing a chain link fence with cut up, disgusting bare feet wasn't exactly thrilling. She scanned the sections of fence, hand over her eyes to shield them from the sun. *There.* "Looks like a tree fell near the corner." Daphne pointed. "We should be able to sneak through."

Together, the three managed to scrabble over a large, hollowed out fir wedged into a long segment of bent and buckled fencing.

As soon as they were inside, Samuel rubbed his palms together, face full of determination. "Alright. Let's see what we can find."

"A whole bunch of nothing, is my guess," Jocelyn noted, worry in her voice plain.

"The little village didn't look like much, either, but we managed to find a bit of food and shelter. Maybe we'll be lucky here, too." Daphne tried to pour as much optimism into her tone as possible.

They approached the hangar, Samuel in the lead, the pair of women trailing behind. He tried the door handle. It wouldn't give. "Locked."

Daphne frowned. The prospect of walking all the way to Ellensburg wasn't in the least appealing. Her feet would give out before she made it even halfway. And Samuel's hip wasn't built for long-haul hikes. Daphne crowded next to Samuel and cupped her hands around her face to peer in the door's window. The sight stole her breath.

Two planes, one a crop duster, the other the little four-seater from the flyer, sat in the hangar, ready and able. She had no idea when they'd been flown last or if they even had any fuel, but they were intact. And it gave them options.

She pulled back. "We need a rock. Something heavy."

"For what?"

"To break this glass." She cast her gaze about, searching. About ten feet away, the asphalt crumbled into larger pieces and she hurried over. With a bit of effort, she wedged her fingers beneath a larger chunk and hauled it up, grunting as it wobbled. "This should do it."

"Are you sure we should—"

Daphne didn't wait for Jocelyn to finish. She threw the chunk of broken asphalt as hard as she dared at the glass. It shattered on impact, breaking into elongated, wicked shards. Samuel motioned for her to stay back. "Let me. I'm the one in boots." He stepped forward and pulled his sleeve down over his hand before knocking the glass out of the frame. He then eased his arm through the open space and unlocked the door from the inside.

"Watch where you step. That door's old enough the glass isn't tempered."

Daphne advanced on the balls of her feet, dodging the shards littering the ground until she stepped onto the cool, smooth hangar floor. On the wall beside them, a handful of keys dangled. She hurried over with Samuel right behind. He used his lighter to illuminate the keychains. Daphne plucked the one for the four-seater off the wall with a grin. "We might be in business."

"I'll figure out how to open the doors." Samuel made his way to the large sliding doors as Daphne and Jocelyn headed toward the plane.

"Are you sure about this?"

Daphne stood beside the plane, thinking over the best answer when a groan of metal-on-metal sounded behind her. The morning light cut across the hangar in a wide arc, lighting up the old plane, its blue paint faded and chipped. It sat there like a relic of another era, dust layered thick on the wings and fuselage. Spider webs crisscrossed the propeller and the windows, making Daphne wonder just how long it had been grounded.

Jocelyn eyed the small aircraft skeptically.

Daphne managed a smile. "Learned to fly on one just like it. Maybe not so dusty, that's all." She tried to exude more confidence than she felt.

Samuel grunted as he circled the plane, his gaze sharp and assessing. "This thing's older than me. Any fuel inside's probably turned to varnish by now."

Daphne nodded. "It won't be a smooth ride." She hauled the door open and climbed inside before inspecting the cockpit, her fingers brushing over the rusty instrument panel. As she took the pilot seat, the leather cracked beneath her.

Jocelyn gingerly boarded, eyeing the worn belt. "Can't believe I'm doing this," she whispered, gripping the sides.

Samuel settled in the back, his veteran eyes scanning the woods outside. "Better rough in the air than stuck on the ground."

Daphne's hand hovered over the ignition momentarily. *I can do this. I have to do this.* She took a deep breath and pulled out the parking brake before checking the throttle, ensuring it was slightly open. With her left hand, she switched on the master switch, bringing the aircraft's electrical system to life.

She checked the fuel gauge — not full, but enough to try.

"Priming the engine," she explained to her passengers. "It needs a little fuel to get started." She reached for the primer knob, giving it three slow pumps to introduce a small amount of fuel directly into the engine.

The radio stack hummed softly, and Daphne took a moment to adjust the frequency, though she wasn't expecting to communicate with anyone. She was just used to the routine.

She then took the ignition key and turned it to the 'START' position. The propeller groaned into motion, sluggish from disuse. The engine sputtered and choked, the old fuel not igniting cleanly. She tried again, holding the key a few seconds longer. The engine roared to life on the third attempt, though it ran unevenly, the sound ragged.

Jocelyn jumped at the abrupt noise, her eyes wide. "Is it supposed to sound like that?"

Samuel laughed from the back, "This old bird's just clearing her throat."

Daphne shot him a grateful glance, adjusting the throttle for a smoother idle. The vibration under her hands felt both familiar and foreign. "Hold on," she cautioned. "We're moving." She slowly eased off the brake and the plane trundled forward, the old wheels crunching over the grassy airfield.

Daphne's grip tightened on the yoke, the plane bouncing lightly on the uneven runway. The plane's engine growled, and its pitch increased as she advanced the throttle, coaxing more power out of the reluctant machine.

"Here goes nothing," she whispered.

The plane began to gain speed, the wheels bumping rapidly beneath them. Daphne pulled back on the yoke, attempting to get the nose up and gain altitude. But the plane didn't respond as she remembered, the stale fuel hampering its performance.

The end of the runway loomed alarmingly close, the trees beyond standing tall and menacing. Panic fluttered in Daphne's chest. She muttered out a curse.

Jocelyn's knuckles blanched where she gripped the seat, and she shot Daphne a wide-eyed look. "Are we—?"

Daphne didn't wait for her to finish. She quickly

pulled back on the throttle, pushing down on the yoke to level the plane. The tires skidded slightly, sending grass and small stones flying as she applied the brakes hard. The aircraft jolted to a stop just shy of the runway's end, the shadow of the trees stretching long and dark over the nose. The engine grumbled, sounding just as shaken as the occupants inside.

For a moment, the only sound was the heavy breathing of the three passengers.

Samuel was the first to break the silence. "Well," he remarked dryly, "that was exhilarating."

Daphne exhaled deeply, her heart racing. "Sorry, that was...not as I remembered."

Jocelyn, her voice shaky, added, "Can we talk about another plan?"

Daphne's jaw set with determination. She wasn't going to fail them. Not when they'd come this far. "I've got this," she insisted. "Just need to shake off the rust."

She began by pulling the throttle back to idle, allowing the engine to purr calmly. Turning her attention to the rudder pedals at her feet, she pressed the left one, gently steering the plane to the left to maneuver it into a turnaround. The tail swung around smoothly, pointing the nose back toward the opposite end of the runway.

As the plane trundled forward, Daphne looked over the gauges again. Fuel levels, oil pressure, airspeed — every indicator received her scrutiny. She could feel the eyes of Jocelyn and Samuel on her, quietly assessing. She tried to lift her own confidence. *I can do this.*

Reaching the starting point of the runway, Daphne

came to a full stop. She took a moment, her hands leaving the controls, to massage her temples and steady her breathing. This was it. She had to trust her training and instincts.

"I just need more speed before attempting to lift," she reasoned aloud. "And a more gradual pull on the yoke."

Samuel nodded in agreement from the back. "Sometimes, slow and steady does the trick."

Taking one last deep breath, Daphne advanced the throttle again. The engine roared in response, and they began their second trek down the runway. This time, her actions were more measured, more deliberate. With every second that passed, hope grew that they might truly take to the skies.

The plane surged forward, the roar of the engine filling the small cabin. Daphne held the throttle firmly, ensuring maximum power, feeling the vibrations of the aircraft through the yoke and the rudder pedals under her feet. The sound of the tires over the grassy runway became a rapid drumbeat, a pulsating rhythm signaling their increasing speed.

She could sense Jocelyn beside her, holding her breath, her body stiff and rigid. Behind, Samuel's presence was a silent but grounding force. Daphne fixed her gaze on the far end of the runway, her mind calculating the distance.

The plane gathered speed, the vibrations growing more intense. The old craft was giving its all. She felt it in her bones, the tingling anticipation of flight. She waited for that sweet spot, the moment the plane was begging to be freed from the ground.

With a gradual pull on the yoke, she asked the plane to rise. Unlike before, she felt the plane respond, the nose tipping up ever so slightly. The tension in the wheels lessened as they skimmed the surface, and then, like a bird stretching its wings for the first time in a long while, the plane lifted.

The ground fell away, the runway shrinking below them. The dense tree line at the end of the field became a blur of green, and they were clear. The climb was not without its jolts and jerks, thanks to the old fuel and the plane's prolonged disuse, but they were airborne.

Daphne let out a shaky breath, her hands still gripping the controls tightly. "We did it," she whispered, her voice filled with relief and awe.

Beside her, Jocelyn laughed, the sound a mix of joy and disbelief.

From the back, Samuel's chuckle carried a note of nostalgia. "Just like old times," he murmured. The horizon stretched before them, vast and open.

After a few moments, Daphne relaxed. The plane was steady in the air. They were actually flying.

Samuel leaned forward. "Keep it steady and low so we can find I-90."

Daphne nodded, her gaze on the controls while Samuel leaned over from the back to inspect the ground below. The vast landscape of Washington state sprawled beneath them. Daphne oriented the plane to the direction of I-90, the highway acting as their lifeline through the wilderness. The majestic Cascade Range flanked the interstate to the west, their snow-capped peaks gleaming against the blue sky. To the east, the semi-arid landscape of the Columbia Plateau stretched out, its gentle undulations casting soft shadows.

Samuel, ever observant, pointed out landmarks from the backseat. "See that river down there? That's the Yakima. We're on the right track."

As they flew, Daphne kept the plane at a steady altitude, adjusting occasionally to avoid the sporadic puff of a small cloud. The drone of the engine was consistent, the earlier spluttering now a distant memory.

After some time, the landscape began to change. The tight grid of roads, neat patches of agricultural land, and the clustering of buildings signaled the outskirts of a town.

"That's got to be it up ahead."

"Are you sure?" Daphne glanced at Samuel in the back.

He nodded. "It's the biggest town around here. Pretty sure the flight time is right."

Daphne turned back around and concentrated again on flying, circling the town a few times, her eyes scanning the ground for an airfield. On the third round, she spotted what she was looking for—a single, narrow runway surrounded by grasslands, with a small building that likely functioned as an office or a control center.

"There," Daphne pointed. "We'll land there."

She adjusted the plane's direction, lining up with the runway. Her eyes constantly darted between the instrument panel and the approaching ground, ensuring her approach angle was just right.

As they descended, the details of the airfield became clearer: the faded runway markings, the windsock billowing to the side, a few parked cars suggesting the presence of people.

"Brace yourselves," Daphne warned, adjusting the throttle, and preparing for the descent. The landing would be the true test of her rusty skills and the plane's old mechanics. She simply had to get this right. She steered across the runway, trying her best to keep the plane straight and level.

Daphne descended with cautious precision, trying to recall the exact feel of landing smoothly. The altimeter's needle ticked downward, the numbers decreasing as the plane made its descent. Her pulse quickened.

She aimed to touchdown near the runway's threshold, but the plane had other ideas. With a gust of wind, it shifted slightly, pushing them off-center. Daphne adjusted, gripping the yoke tighter. The wheels brushed the tarmac with a screech, bouncing once before fully making contact. The old brakes groaned in protest as she applied them, the plane jerking forward in a series of jolts.

It was hard, abrupt, nothing like the textbook landings of her training days. But they were on solid ground. The aircraft slowed, eventually coming to a full stop midway down the runway. Its engine idled for a moment before Daphne turned it off, the sudden silence echoing in their ears.

She exhaled heavily, her shoulders slumping. "Not my best landing," she admitted, her voice tinged with embarrassment.

Jocelyn, despite being a little shaken, managed a wry smile. "But we're in one piece, right? And we didn't have to walk here."

"Any landing you can walk away from is a good one," Samuel added.

Daphne let a small laugh slip from between her lips. "Then by that measure, we did great." She unbuckled her seatbelt, taking a moment to appreciate solid ground beneath her. They had made it.

"Guys?"

Daphne turned as Jocelyn pointed out the window.

Men in military uniforms swarmed the plane on all sides, rifles up, barrels pointing at their faces.

CHAPTER FOURTEEN
CLINT

"How are you holding up, sweetheart?" Clint paused in the hike and swiveled when he noticed Mika was no longer walking along beside him.

She trudged a few feet behind now. Her cheeks were red from exertion. Her hair was coming out of her ponytail and her shirt was hanging off one shoulder, slipping down the top part of her arm. Her feet shuffled like sludge across the bed of leaves, and she studied the ground as if she feared it would open and swallow her whole.

"Mika?" Clint asked again, concern for her wellbeing bubbling to the surface of his mind again.

"Hmm?" Mika lifted her head and gave Clint an absent stare.

"Are you ok? Do you need to take a break?"

Mika scratched the back of her head and lifted her gaze to the canopy of pines overhead. They had found a trailhead near the road and were currently using the colored markers they found on the tree trunks every so often as their guide along the path.

This area was dense with trees, and only a few patches of sunlight were allowed in from the cloak of forest. It was chillier, even though it was early summer, but Mika looked flushed.

"I'm alright," she shrugged.

Clint frowned, skeptical. He knew she had to be tired and hungry, if not parched. Clint's throat was dry, and his tongue was as gritty as if he'd just chewed a clump of sand and swallowed it.

To say they needed water was an understatement. He was running on fumes, but he knew it had to be ten times worse for Mika. Along the way, Clint had been looking out for anything they could eat, like recognizable berries that would be safe to consume, anything they could put in their stomachs to keep them going. But the spring had been colder, and it had taken a while for the snow and the frigid temperatures to thaw, which left little forageable food for them to pick through in the wilderness.

They ambled on. A few minutes later, Clint heard the familiar rush of running water. He looked over at Mika, allowing her time to catch up.

"Do you hear it?" he asked.

Mika tilted her head and concentrated. Clint saw it register in her face as it lit up. Her eyes went wide. "Water?"

"A stream, perhaps." Clint smiled, Mika's eagerness rubbing off on him.

Even Mika picked up the pace. Another minute ticked by and they saw the stream near a clearing in the woods.

"Yes!" Mika practically purred. She dropped her backpack to the ground and tried to jog toward the water, but it was more of a hobble.

"Mika, wait," Clint said, and she turned around.

"What is it?"

"I don't know if that water is safe to drink."

"Dad," she whimpered. Her shoulders sank. "I can't take it any longer. I'm going to die if I don't have water."

Clint knew it was true. He wasn't going to be able to resist either.

"Alright, we'll drink it, but we have to be prepared that it might make us sick."

Mika went to her knees beside the bank and cupped her hands under the water. "It's *ice* cold," she shrieked with excitement.

She brought her cupped hands to her lips and greedily slurped at the water. He knelt beside her. She pressed her palms into the dirt and stuck her whole mouth into the water, not bothering to use her hands. She lapped at it like a thirsty dog would take to a bowl.

"Easy does it," Clint advised her. "Just take it slow. There's plenty."

Mika drank for several more minutes before she backed away, looking satisfied, if not slightly dazed. "Now all I need is a greasy cheeseburger with curly fries and a huge strawberry milkshake."

Clint's own stomach rumbled at the fantasy—but that's all it could be for now.

"I don't think we'll find any of those things out here in the woods, but I'm with you."

After a long rest at the creek side, they resumed their trek, following the trail until it opened into a campground.

Mika halted in her tracks and held up a hand. Alarm buzzed through Clint's bones and his stomach dropped out.

"What's wrong?"

"Do you hear that?" Mika whispered.

Clint's ears pricked and he strained to listen.

A peal of laughter filtered through the cedars. A woman's voice, then a man responding. Then a child's giggle.

"Is that a kid?" Mika asked, her eyebrows quirking up.

"Sounds like it."

"Should we check it out?"

"Let's just keep walking and see what happens."

They slowed their stride, and after a bend, a huge orange and gray tent perched alongside the trail. Mika stopped and instinctively walked to stand behind Clint.

He gave her a wary glance and took an apprehensive step forward. There was a fire going in a fire pit with smoke snaking up to the treetops in a long, silver coil.

There were two kayaks sitting beside the tent, one dark blue and one orange, like the tent. A clothing line hung between two cedars, and a few shirts and a pair of pink child-sized shorts were hung at the end. A purple set of small galoshes sat next to the tent on the other side.

Clint tried to ease his mind. If there were children here, maybe they wouldn't have to worry about a violent or hostile encounter.

A woman with wavy chestnut hair had her back to Clint and Mika. She was holding something over the fire, as if to dry it.

"John, your socks got wet when Madison spilled her juice on them," she called out.

"That's okay, honey," a male voice came from inside the tent.

A young girl with blonde pigtails jumped at the edge of the stream.

The woman, assumingly the mother, called out to the girl. "Madison, sweetie, don't play over there without your rain boots on. You'll catch a cold."

Clint eased Mika's pack off his chest and set it on the ground before hiding the rifle behind it. He didn't want to scare this family first thing.

A teenage boy with a mop of curly light-brown hair read a book in one of the camping chairs that encircled the campfire. He lifted his head at the noise of Clint and the pack and stood up, calling attention to himself. His mother turned around and finally spotted them.

"Hello." Clint's weak voice echoed through the trees. He lifted a hand and tossed them a friendly wave. "How are you folks doing?"

To his surprise, the woman's eyes brightened, and a warm smile spread across her lips.

"Hey there," she called out. "Enjoying a hike on this beautiful day?"

Clint looked over at Mika. Her chin wrinkled and began to tremble as if she was holding back a sob. It sent a surge of emotions quivering through Clint, but he held them back.

"Well, you could say that." He released a crackly laugh and stepped forward.

The woman's expression changed, noticing Mika's emotional distress.

A man with hair the same flaxen color as his daughter's emerged from the tent. The open flaps billowed in the gentle breeze.

He stood up straight, giving Clint a quizzical gaze. "Afternoon," he called out. "You folks look a bit out of sorts. Are you lost?"

Mika sniffled and wiped her damp cheek with the corner of her shirt sleeve.

The man frowned. "Everything alright?"

The young daughter with the pigtails noticed the new arrivals and started walking back to the campsite, her hair bouncing at her shoulders.

"It's been a rough few days, to be honest." Clint's voice broke, betraying his stress.

"What happened?" The woman's face flashed with concern. "Are you hurt? We don't have cell service out here, but we can try to help you if we're able."

Clint offered her a kind smile. "That means a lot to me." He looked at Mika. "To us."

Mika chewed on her bottom lip as tears escaped her lower lash line and dribbled down her cheek.

The woman's eyes panned between them, and a crease formed between her brows.

"I'm Clint, and this is my daughter, Mika. We have been trying to get to Ellensburg. It's where we're trying to find her mother, my..." he trailed off, unable to bring himself to say the words ex-wife.

"We're from there," The man brightened, but a moment later, confusion knit his brows. "Wait, I don't understand. Did she get lost on the trail?" The man stepped closer. "I'm John, by the way. My wife, Susan. Our children," he gestured to the teen son, "Michael and Madison."

"Nice to meet you," Clint said.

Mika gave a polite nod beside him.

"She was in Bellevue when everything—" Clint began to explain.

The woman and the man both stared at him, uncomprehending.

"What *everything*?" Susan asked. "Did something happen?"

Clint raised a single eyebrow, his words coming out flat and slow. "The... earthquake...tsunami?"

Susan gasped. Her hand went to her mouth, and her eyes went as wide as dinner plates. "What—what are you talking about?"

Clint exchanged a hesitant glance with his daughter. "How long have you all been out here?"

"We live in eastern Washington," Susan offered. "We've been camping here for nearly a week now."

He closed his eyes for a long moment and pinched the bridge of his nose. They actually didn't know. He explained the situation slowly, glossing over the terrors they'd endured leading up to finding their campsite.

"There were no tremors through here?" Mika asked, speaking for the first time since they'd arrived to the group.

Susan shook her head. "No, nothing."

"So—Seattle—it's really—underwater?" Michael asked, his eyes blinking, his mouth hanging open in shock.

"Most of it was, at least." Clint explained. "Although the water's receded quite a bit by now."

"You must be starving." Susan hurried to a picnic table that had a pop up tent over it, and a protective bug net clasped around each of the four cornered sides. "Here, I've got extra water." She handed two bottles out through the opening in the screen.

"Are you hungry? I was going to start cooking some burgers and dogs over the fire," John offered.

Clint began to salivate. "We don't want to impose—"

"When was the last time you ate a hearty meal?" Susan interrupted.

Mika answered for them both. "A long time." Her voice broke on the last word and Susan hurried out of the screened tent, arms open. Mika folded into them like a crumpled piece of paper. Susan patted her on the back.

The sight lodged a knot in Clint's throat and he swallowed hard to clear it.

"It's alright. You are welcome to stay and eat with us, regain your energy. We're happy to help in any way we can."

Mika pulled away and wiped her eyes with the back of her hand. "Thank you so much," she squeaked.

John set to work on the burgers and hot dogs. The smell wafted through the air, sending Clint's hunger into a tailspin. Mika eased down to the ground to sit.

"Do you want to color with me?" The little girl stood a few steps away, eyes lifted and hopeful.

"Maddie, sweetie, I'm sure she's tired." Susan gave her daughter a sidelong look.

"I don't mind." Mika smiled at the little girl and her whole face burst into a grin before she scurried away to get her supplies.

"She loves to color." Michael, the teenager, sat down next to Mika. Clint smiled at his feeble attempt at being subtle, an excuse to talk to a girl close in age. "So, how old are you?"

"Sixteen."

"That's cool. Me too. Sophomore?"

"Yep." Mika nodded. Clint noticed a sliver of a smile trying to tug at the edges of her lips. He was grateful they had stumbled upon this kind and accommodating family.

"Alright, who wants what?" John called out, spatula in hand. Susan was bringing out the ketchup and mustard from the cooler. She set it on the table, along with paper plates.

"We have mess kits, but not enough. I hope this is alright," she said to Clint.

"It's more than alright,' he admitted.

Mika stood up and when she did, so did Michael. He slipped his hands into his pockets, as Clint noted, trying to be casual and smooth. "I can get your food for you, if you want to just sit down and relax?"

Clint smiled.

"No, that's alright," Mika glanced at her dad. "I can get it."

They sat down around the campfire to eat, kids on the ground, Clint on the edge of a fallen log, the parents in camping chairs. Clint dug into his food in silence, relishing the taste of something warm and filling.

After a few minutes, he glanced over again at his daughter. She was deep in conversation with Michael about bands they liked in common. He was grateful she was distracted, but the sky was turning gray overhead, and soon dusk would settle in over the forest like a cloak. He worried about going forward into the night, but at least they'd have food fuel to keep them going.

As if reading his mind, Susan leaned toward him from her chair. "We can all huddle in as a family in the big tent tonight if you want to use the one for the kids. It sleeps two, it will be perfect for you and Mika. We have extra sets of blankets and pillows, too."

Clint swallowed down his bite of hamburger and tried not to choke. "Are you sure?"

"Absolutely!" She chimed and swatted her hand

through the air. "Right, John?" She looked at her husband sitting on the other side of the crackling fire.

He nodded, his hand at his mouth as he chewed. "Stay as long as you need. We have plenty."

They fell into easy conversation, Clint explaining where they were from, what they knew of the chaos and destruction in Seattle and the surrounding areas. Susan and John shared their own history and how they'd gotten into camping as a family a few years ago. How important it was for them to go off-grid and recharge.

The more they talked, the more Clint relaxed, the tension he'd held so tight the last several days slackening by the hour.

Clint glanced overhead as he heard a faint drone from the sky. Looking up, he spotted a small plane. Its engine sounded a touch ragged, hinting at its age and the strain of its journey. For a moment, as the plane's shadow skimmed over the campsite, he thought of meeting Daphne all those years ago, before Mika was even a thought in either of their minds.

He watched the plane until it was no more than a speck in the distance, its engine noise fading. With any luck, Daphne was safe in Ellensburg and they would be there soon, reuniting. He would finally be able to look into her eyes and see her face, to have the chance to tell her how much he wanted to give their life together another shot.

"Show us your hands!" A man in utilities pointed at Daphne with his rifle. His cover shielded his eyes from view, but the set of his jaw was firm and unyielding.

Daphne lifted her hands by her sides. Jocelyn whimpered beside her.

Samuel raised his arms and called out from the back seat. "We don't mean any harm, sir."

"Why didn't you respond to air control?" The guard addressed his question to Daphne sitting in the pilot's seat.

"The—the radio doesn't work," she stammered.

The guard stepped forward in a shuffling motion as he kept the rifle trained on her center mass. "Were you aware this entire area is restricted access?"

"What? No. We're—" Daphne turned back to glance at Samuel. When she hesitated, the guard reached up and yanked the door open. Daphne recoiled.

Another soldier advanced, gun trained on her, as the

one who'd done the talking slung his rifle behind him and reached out. He wrapped his hand around her arm and tugged, half pulling her out of the plane's seat.

"Wait, stop, ouch—I can do it," she finally pleaded. "Please, I'll cooperate. We all will."

The soldier stepped back, allowing Daphne, Samuel, and Jocelyn to step out from the plane. The three of them huddled together trembling, almost cowering, as the soldiers surrounded them in a half-circle.

"Where did you find out about this airstrip?" The one seemingly in charge spoke again.

"We—we didn't," Daphne stammered. "We just found it from the air. We were looking for a place to land."

"Why here?"

"We were trying to reach Ellensburg. The large FEMA shelter." Daphne wrung her hands together. "That's where we are, right? We guessed right?" Tears welled behind her eyes, blurring her vision.

"Why there?"

"My husband and daughter are there. They were looking for me in Bellevue, but they went to the shelter hoping I'd be there. We all survived—" She glanced at her friends. "The quake and the water and were trying to reach the shelter when our bus crashed—"

"Was attacked," Samuel interjected.

"Right." Daphne swallowed and kept talking, rushing the words out. "We were attacked so we didn't want to ride another one, so we set off in a truck, but then it ran out of gas and—"

The soldier held up a hand. "So you're refugees."

"Y—yes."

For the first time, the man looked her over, gaze pausing for a long moment on her dirty, bloodstained feet. "And you escaped the quake and the tsunami."

She tried to smooth down a tangled clump of hair. "Yes."

"Do you have any weapons?"

"No." Daphne shook her head. "We don't even have food."

"Or shoes," Samuel offered.

"Alright." The soldier motioned for everyone to lower their rifles. Jocelyn visibly relaxed beside Daphne as the men around them eased.

"Hawthorne, get a people hauler and escort these civilians to the Ellensburg triage area."

"Yes, sir." One of the men a few steps away turned and began to jog across the airstrip.

"Where are we going?" Jocelyn squeaked.

"We'll transport you via a National Guard vehicle to intake at Ellensburg." He paused for a long moment, appraising their sorry state again. "Looks like you all could do with some medical treatment."

"What about the plane?"

He glanced at it. "Does it fly?"

"Barely."

"We'll move it out of the way for now. You can retrieve it later."

Daphne glanced at Jocelyn as she tugged on her lip with her teeth. The other woman shook her head briefly and Daphne nodded. Telling them they'd stolen the plane would only complicate matters. After all this, after she found Clint and Mika and a pair of shoes, maybe she could bring it to a FEMA employee's attention.

Or maybe not.

She glanced back at the plane one last time as a pair of soldiers escorted them to a large military transport vehicle with benches in the back and a camouflage fabric cover. She climbed aboard and Jocelyn took a seat beside her. Samuel sat opposite and a soldier climbed in last.

The engine revved to life and sent a promising vibration jogging through Daphne's bones. She stared out the back opening as the truck began to move. She was dog-tired, and her rational thoughts were starting to dissolve. She imagined herself in a jetted tub with warm water and sudsy bubbles filling it to the brim, a warm glass of Pinot Noir in one hand and a good book in the other.

It sounded like heaven. She had to isolate herself into the deepest fantasies of her mind in order to survive the reality of her present. Every flex and move of her feet sent pain poking and prodding into her flesh. Her shoulders ached from the strain of landing the plane. She couldn't say how long they were in the vehicle, but it was evening by the time they reached the refugee station.

Dust rose in plumes from the vehicle's giant tires, turning the air gritty and dense. Daphne coughed, the taste of dirt and exhaustion catching in her throat. They had finally arrived.

A soldier helped her down from the giant truck and

she winced as her bare feet contacted the ground. People milled everywhere. Soldiers, National Guard, she now supposed, were standing about, some watching with careful eyes, others helping keep order in lines. To her left, a large canvas sign read "Processing" with an arrow pointing towards a series of tables where staff, identifiable by their bright vests, checked in new arrivals.

A snaking line of tired and weary refugees waited their turn. Some leaned on makeshift crutches, others sat on their packed belongings, exhaustion evident in their posture. The murmurs of the crowd, a blend of anxiety and relief, filled the air.

Twenty feet past the line, a row of porta-potties huddled together at the edge of well-trodden grass. A trio of children, all barefoot and grubby, chased each other across the thin strip of lawn, their laughter a stark contrast to their surroundings.

A haggard looking man with a cane hobbled past them. A woman with a dazed gleam in her eye pushed the wheelchair of an elderly woman wearing a dirty nightgown.

The quake and the tsunami had been disastrous and unimaginable in their strength and horror. But this sea of humanity, desperate and in need, was overwhelming. Daphne stumbled and flailed her arm to keep from falling.

"You all right?" Jocelyn leaned closer and took her hand.

"I—I guess I didn't expect—"

"It to be like this?" Jocelyn shook her head. "Neither did I."

They walked toward the line together with Samuel following behind. They stopped at what they hoped was the end of the line and Daphne took it all in, dumbfounded, appalled, and stunned. There were so many people in desperate need of food, water, medicine, stitches, showers. The list of needs was endless, and the demand was too high to handle any of it quickly or well.

Daphne was just one of hundreds, if not thousands, of people in dire need of care and services. There were too many to keep track of, and more continued to filter in by the dozen—just like they had. Behind them, the line only grew and grew.

A woman in blue scrubs stumbled out from the tent. Her cheeks were red, eyes ringed in dark circles. She tugged her scrubs cap off and crumpled it in her hand as she sucked in a deep breath, leaning on the pole of the tent for support. Whatever she'd seen or endured inside, it had been too much.

Daphne inhaled.

A few spots ahead stood a family of four. The father, a tall man with a once-sturdy build, now seemed gaunt, his cheekbones sharply pronounced under a week's worth of unshaven stubble. His shirt, once bright blue, was now dulled by layers of dust and sweat, and clung to his frame. One of his arms cradled a plastic container – perhaps once filled with cherished family photos or documents – now guarding their remaining essentials.

Beside him, a woman with a long ratty braid of

chestnut hair tried to soothe their youngest, a toddler with big hazel eyes. The child's lips were chapped, his tiny fingers clutching a threadbare stuffed rabbit. His small face, smeared with dirt, occasionally buried itself into the crook of his mother's neck, seeking comfort.

The eldest, a girl of about ten, stood protectively close to her younger brother. In her hands was a water bottle, nearly empty. She'd periodically unscrew the cap, tilt the bottle, and coax a single drop onto her brother's lips. Her own lips were parched and cracked, but Daphne never saw her drink.

The way they huddled close, the silent exchanges of glances between the parents, and the almost mechanical motions of care, all hinted at a journey fraught with challenges. They spoke little, but their eyes, heavy with a mix of fatigue and hope, conveyed more than words ever could. The physical weariness was evident, but it was the silent weight of their ordeal that left the deepest impression.

Daphne turned in slow motion and stared all around her. There were countless other families, some in better shape, some worse. All in desperate need.

A man wearing a FEMA shirt almost stumbled directly into Daphne, sidestepping her at the last second on his march toward the front of the line.

As they crept forward, a small commotion caught Daphne off guard.

"Please," a middle-aged woman with a mixture of silver and blonde hair cried, lifting her hands into prayer position as she practically groveled at the boots of a soldier standing near the tent. "You have to tell me if my son has been through here. I know his name must be on a list somewhere."

The soldier, not unkindly, but firmly, shook his head. A hint of remorse flitted through his eyes. "I'm sorry ma'am, this one goes over my head. I don't have access to any of the intake lists. You'll have to go through processing just like everyone else."

The woman's shoulders collapsed, and her head sunk deep into her hands as she sobbed. Daphne's eyes misted and she tore her gaze away.

Jocelyn squeezed her hand. "I know it looks bad, but it's got to be better inside. All we have to do is hold on, get through the line, and then we'll get some help."

"She's right," Samuel offered behind them. "We stay here, wait our turn, and it'll all work out."

Daphne inhaled a shaky breath and hoped her friends were right.

Cherise McNeil squinted at the screen. It had been eight days since the earthquake and tsunami ravaged the Pacific Northwest and McNeil hadn't slept more than a handful of hours at a time throughout. The video feed on the computer screen in front of her stuttered, then froze momentarily. Faces blinked back, expressions of concern and exhaustion in pixelated form.

She closed her eyes briefly and rubbed the fatigue from the bridge of her nose. On the screen, men began to file into a conference room at the White House. Michael Urston, the head of FEMA, shuffled in, a stack of papers clutched in his hand. The Governors of Washington and Oregon sat at the ready, the weight of the disaster wearing deep creases in their wrinkled faces.

"Morning, everyone," Urston offered. "Now that we're all here, let's get started. Governor, I think you offered to begin?"

The Governor of Oregon straightened, his elbow

resting on the desk. "I know everyone's been asking for numbers. I finally have some initial estimates."

"Go ahead."

The Governor ran his free hand across his growing stubble – not a style choice, Cherise knew, but a mark of exhaustion, of relentless days and sleepless nights.

"Oregon's coastal population," he started, voice heavy, "about twenty-two percent are aged sixty-five or over. Twenty-nine percent is disabled."

"How many were in the inundation zone?" The Chairman of the Joint Chiefs of Staff interrupted.

A brief pause as he consulted his notes. "71,000." A shadow passed over his features. "Based on reports coming in from the FEMA relief tents, we are guessing most didn't survive."

A palpable, mournful silence settled. Cherise sank back, eyes distant. Grief hung in the virtual space, pressing on each participant.

"We've heard reports that many people are unaware of the main processing facility in Ellensburg and the ones who are, well—" He paused for a long moment. "Are having trouble reaching it."

"We've heard the same," Governor Peters interjected, hand ruffling his hair. "Roads are either completely jammed or destroyed. Towns on the way are overrun with refugees. Many are running out of gas and food. Residents are fed up with the incoming hordes."

Governor Griffin nodded. "It's the same in Oregon. People are giving up, deciding to camp out in their cars in these little towns just outside the disaster zone. The residents are overwhelmed. Local restaurants have lines half a mile long and they're running out of food. The local grocery stores are bare. Gas stations empty. If we don't get these people to move on, we're going to have civil unrest."

Urston's head bobbed. "We're aware of the issues and are exploring alternatives."

"Like?" Peters queried.

"Radio broadcasts on every over-the-air channel. Satellite radio, as well. Local TV ads," Cherise chimed in. "It's not perfect, but we're trying to push the information out there."

Peters shifted, restless. "It's not a full solution."

Cherise met his gaze, resolute. "Never said it was."

"We're united in this," Urston said sharply, aiming to cut the mounting tension. "Our goal is to help everyone—not just the displaced citizens, but those providing aid and comfort."

"Is Ellensburg even fully operational?" Peters asked. "I'm getting reports from my constituents of long lines, sometimes overnight, and a lack of food and water. Not enough shelters. That people are either being turned away or asked to move on before they've even had a chance to take a shower or change their clothes."

Cherise inhaled sharply. Ellensburg was under tremendous strain, that was true. But they were doing their best with the resources at their disposal. "We could use some additional support from the National Guard to move supplies and keep the peace."

Peters snorted and shook his head. "I told you days

ago we couldn't spare any more. Didn't Montana and Idaho send troops? Isn't that enough?"

Cherise counted to five before responding. "Neighboring states have reached out, but they've been slow to respond. As of yet, no additional assistance has arrived."

The Chairman cleared his throat. "The 82nd Airborne Division ready brigade is en route. We are also in the process of mobilizing regiments from Camp Pendleton and Twenty-nine Palms."

"Where will these troops be stationed?"

"We're converting the Yakima Training Area to a Base Support Installation to liaison with FEMA and other emergency organizations. All troops will deploy from and be stationed there. It'll be operational as long as needed."

"And these troops will do what, exactly?" Peters, again.

"FEMA support will be the priority."

Urston nodded. "We've been in contact with the Commanding General of the 82nd and are gearing up to deploy those troops to Ellensburg and the relief tents closer to the disaster zone. They'll move supplies and provide security as needed."

Peters leaned back in his chair. "Does that mean Ellensburg will be secure? Orderly? Will people actually get the help they need?"

"As you're aware, Governor—" The Chairman began.

"Don't patronize me," Peters shot back. "You want Washington residents—my people—to head to a processing facility that you can't guarantee will do a damn thing to help them. Forgive me if I want a little more than *we're working on it.*"

"We all have the same goal, Peters," the Chairman shot back, voice rising.

Cherise's pulse quickened, the air around her growing thick. Anticipation, like a storm cloud, gathered. Every word exchanged was a potential spark, every glance a precursor to lightning. She could almost hear the distant rumble of a storm, the tension palpable, her mind racing for solutions as the weight of potential conflict bore down on them. She had to dispel the tension.

She leaned forward and spoke over the men. "I'm sure as soon as my people at Ellensburg speak to the commanding officer of the 82nd Airborne, we can come up with a solution we're all satisfied with."

Governor Peters resisted, head shaking on the screen. "We need more than that. We need a guarantee."

"Which I'm sure we can give you in a few days." She tried to smile, but the man was having none of it. She knew Peters. He was reasonable. A good person deep down. But he'd been pushed to his limit over this disaster.

Washington residents were injured, hungry, exhausted, and homeless. He was right, they needed more. She wished she could snap her fingers and deliver. But emergency management often worked painfully slow. Things always got worse before they got better.

After a moment, Peters threw up his hands and stood up. He stalked off screen.

The call continued without him as Urston ran down

a list of updates. Cherise attempted to stay focused, but her mind was on the Ellensburg facility and Peters' valid criticisms. Until more processing facilities opened, it would be congested and substandard and maybe even dangerous. But they would turn things around with the military's help.

Pain throbbed behind her eyes as she ended the call. She stared upward for a long moment, hope mingling with doubt.

CHAPTER SEVENTEEN
CLINT

At dawn, John and Susan began packing their supplies. Susan, with a warmth in her eyes, insisted on whipping up a generous serving of bacon, eggs, and richly buttered toast on the skillet. Clint appreciated the gesture deeply, a moment of normalcy amid the chaos of the past week. Mika's enthusiasm mirrored his as she devoured her plate, taking large, hungry bites.

"Need help with the tents?" Clint asked John, rolling up his sleeves.

John hesitated, but after Clint practically begged to help, he relented. "Only if you're up for it. Take it easy, okay?"

There was an undeniable concern in both John and Susan's eyes for Clint and Mika. John's frequent reminders about not pushing too hard and how his son, Michael, could handle most of the heavy lifting were testament to that. But Clint didn't want to just stand idle. These people had extended such kindness to him and

Mika. He needed to contribute, to return the favor even in the smallest of ways.

Their plan was to journey with John's family, who had agreed to bring them along to their home on the edge of Ellensburg.

"Thank you," Clint repeated often, feeling the weight of gratitude each time. Both John and Susan waved his thanks away, insisting they'd expect the same kindness if roles were reversed.

Clint met their gaze with unwavering certainty as he loaded their bags and the guardsman's rifle into the back of the van. "I would. Without a second thought."

As they settled in, Clint focused on Mika. Every twitch, every color change on her face, reminded him of how she'd barely survived. She'd been through so much, and here she was, sandwiched next to Maddie, a girl untouched by the trauma they'd faced.

Bursting with innocence, the little girl nudged close to Mika, eyes shining. "Wanna play Uno?" she asked, pulling cards from her backpack.

Mika shot Clint a brief, uncertain smile before answering. "Sure, but I warn you, I'm good."

Maddie grinned, her enthusiasm undimmed. "Me too!"

From the front, John reminded, "Maddie, seatbelt on."

Maddie sighed but clicked her seatbelt into place, quickly dealing cards to Mika with practiced ease. Clint turned to the window, lost in thought, as the van's engine rumbled to life. Everywhere he looked, memories surfaced—of their home, his job, and especially Daphne. Was she at the shelter facility? Was she even okay?

From behind, Maddie's cheerful voice pierced his spiraling thoughts. It dragged up memories of a younger Mika, full of childlike wonder. Now, at just sixteen, she wore the weary face of someone thrust too quickly into adulthood. The quake had stolen her carefree days, replacing them with shadows of trauma that Clint feared might never lift.

Clint's thoughts danced between Mika and Daphne. How was his daughter ever going to recover from this? Even if they found her mother, even if they were all reunited, would she ever be the same carefree, confident girl she used to be?

Yes, she would. With a shake of his head he flung off the doubt. No matter what, Clint would make sure his daughter recovered physically, mentally, emotionally. The quake and tsunami might have taken their home and her best friend, but it wouldn't take her spirit.

The van puttered along the gravel road out of the campground and onto a surface street. John headed toward I-90, following the signs. As they reached the highway's entrance, the scene changed dramatically. Cars stood bumper-to-bumper, a seemingly unending stretch of red brake lights.

John's hands, precise on the wheel, loosened a bit. "Didn't see this coming," he murmured, sharing a bewildered look with Susan.

The morning sun illuminated her confusion.

"Bizarre," she responded, a hint of worry tinting her voice.

Mika's eyes met Clint's. They both understood the chaos too well. The recent days had given them their fill.

Up ahead, FEMA buses like the one Clint and Mika chose not to board sat idling, flanked by what appeared to be National Guard vehicles.

Mika spotted them as well and brightened. "Dad," she ventured, sitting a little taller, "aren't those the same buses from the relief tent? Maybe Mom did reach Ellensburg already."

"I don't know, sweetie," he replied carefully, not wanting to feed false hope. "But I hope she did."

A muffled cry sounded outside their vehicle and John pressed the button to roll his window down. As the seal broke, distressed voices wrapped around the van. Clint swiveled in his seat, searching for the source. It didn't take long.

A man wove between the cars ahead. Broad-shouldered and clad in a black hoodie, he brandished a pistol at the closest car. Clint couldn't make out his words, but they were harsh and mean. The man tapped the pistol on the glass before pointing it at the driver. After a moment, the window rolled down and a hand thrust out. The man grabbed whatever was offered and shoved it in the pocket of his hoodie before moving on.

As the man closed in on their van, adrenaline surged in Clint. He whispered urgently to Mika, "Pass me the M4 from the back."

Before she could move, the man was at their window,

thrusting the pistol inside, straight at John. John's hands shot up, shaking. Clint could see the raw fear in his eyes. This kind-hearted man wasn't built for confrontations like this.

"Money, food, now!" The man's voice was rough, demanding. A bag hung by his side, already bulging with stolen goods.

John's voice wavered, "S-Susan, give him your ring. I... I don't have any cash. Will that suffice?"

Susan was in the midst of pulling off her ring when Clint's assertive voice halted her. "No."

Wide-eyed and taken aback, Susan froze, her gaze darting between the menacing man and Clint.

"Do it now," the man snarled, gun still aimed.

"You're not taking a thing," Clint's voice rang out, unwavering. Memories of past ordeals and the losses they'd endured, fueled his conviction. His daughter wasn't getting traumatized again by some bully with a gun. Neither were these good people. He'd had just about enough of the weak side of humanity. He called out even louder, "Move on."

Mika, sensing the mounting tension, shoved the rifle toward her father. He reached for it without looking and hauled it toward the front.

"Clint," John began, his voice a blend of caution and pleading, glancing anxiously at Clint in the rearview mirror, "maybe there's another way—"

"There isn't," Clint countered, determination evident. This only went one way and Clint knew it. The man stepped closer, gun barrel now pointed squarely at Clint. A closer look at him revealed startling truths. Sunken cheeks. Wrinkle-free skin. His eyes, though brimming with misguided defiance, bore the unmistakable mark of youth. The kid was no older than Michael or Mika.

With swift resolve, Clint cracked open the van door. John and Susan's panicked voices surged in protest, fearing the worst, but Clint ignored them. He emerged, rifle in both hands, and pointed it across the hood at the young man.

"Listen closely," Clint started, eyes unwavering. "You leave us alone and rethink your strategy. Waving that gun around is a dangerous gamble."

The young man's eyes darted between Clint and the rifle, then over to John and Susan, a glimmer of doubt evident in his gaze.

"Think for a moment. We're all worn out, all hungry. But we weren't out here, threatening anyone."

"Yeah? Well you look super cozy in there, one big happy family." The kid practically sneered. "Wha'do I got? A whole lotta nothin'."

"That's not true. You're alive. You've already got whatever's filling that bag slung over your shoulder. Isn't that enough?"

Though the kid kept his weapon poised, his posture slumped and his expression softened. "Yeah? So?"

Clint tried again, keeping his tone firm, but controlled. "I get it, you're struggling. So is everyone right now. But threats? This isn't the way. Think about the consequences. You have years ahead of you. Choices matter."

The young man shuffled his feet and the gun dipped in his hand as if the weight grew heavy.

"Really think this through." Clint nodded at the rifle. "I know how to use this. Even if you get a shot off, I will, too. Make the smart decision."

The tension was palpable. Both Clint and the young man locked eyes, gauging each other's resolve. As the seconds ticked on, Clint noted the kid's grip on the gun loosening. *Almost there.*

He motioned with the rifle towards the desert Humvees idling a few hundred yards up the road. "See those military vehicles ahead? You think they won't notice this little scene? Think about the next steps, kid."

Finally, Clint's words reached the young man. He pocketed the pistol and backed away a few paces before turning around and taking off. He wove through the stalled traffic, putting distance between him and the van. Clint waited until he could barely make out the shape of him before lowering the rifle.

As Clint returned to the van, he felt the weight of the passengers' stares. They looked at him, some with gratitude, others with disbelief. Mika, however, simply looked down, clutching Maddie tight beside her.

In the adrenaline's aftermath, Clint's mind raced. Had he pushed too hard? Would the kid come back with reinforcements? But there wasn't room for doubt; he had to protect his daughter and the generous strangers who had taken them in. Still, he couldn't shake the guilt of possibly pushing that young man further down a desperate path.

But it was over. And Mika and this kind family were safe. He exhaled and grabbed the seat belt over his shoulder before turning back to John. "The moment it's possible, take a different route. You've got to get off the main road. We're sitting ducks."

John simply nodded, recognizing the finality in Clint's voice.

A shaft of sun cut across Daphne's face and she blinked her crusted-over eyes open. At some point in the early hours of the morning, the line had officially stopped moving. FEMA employees had walked back and forth, one holding a stack of threadbare blankets, one a meager cart laden with tiny water bottles. They'd apologized. Commiserated. And told them they'd start up processing again in the daylight. If it weren't for the National Guard, the entire line would have erupted into chaos.

Daphne stood on stiff legs and stretched her back. She'd slept on and off, but not well, unconsciousness interrupted by pockets of activity: a child wailing, a skirmish by the porta-potties, a guardsman barking orders.

Beside her, Jocelyn stirred, groaning as she peeled her face off the dirt. "This has got to be a joke, right? One of those gag shows on YouTube? Cause I cannot believe I just spent the night curled up on some nasty patch of ground smellin' pee and man stink all night."

Samuel chuckled as he struggled to stand, but it turned into a cough. Daphne reached out to help him, but he waved her off. "I'm all right. Just slow in the morning. Arthritis in the hip."

About twenty feet ahead, voices rose in a crescendo of anger. A woman, pointing at a smaller group being ushered to the front, shouted, "Why are they skipping the line? We've been here forever!" The accusation resonated with the crowd, and soon more joined her outcry. "It's not right!" yelled another. Distrust bubbled up, turning the atmosphere from weary resignation to volatile resentment.

Jocelyn murmured, "Looks like trouble's brewing." Daphne sighed heavily, longing for this ordeal to be over. Samuel, always alert, edged closer to the two women, ready to protect if needed.

The accuser jabbed a finger into the air. "Been here for hours, and you think you can just waltz up?"

A woman with a tired toddler on her hip chimed in, her voice strained, "Yeah, we've all been waiting! No skipping!"

Across from them, a young woman, her hand on the shoulder of a young man, shot back, "He was just helping that old lady!" She gestured toward an elderly woman a few feet away, who looked disoriented, her skin pale.

"That doesn't give him a free pass!" another man shouted, pointing accusingly.

Amid the commotion, a teenager stepped forward, "I

saw him! He was right here before! He helped her when she stumbled."

As the verbal exchange intensified, the lines of division grew clear, and the once orderly queue began to fracture.

Jocelyn turned to Daphne, her expression grim. "Here we go," she whispered, her fingers twitching nervously around her braids.

Samuel, attempting to mediate, stepped slightly forward. "Everyone! Let's keep calm," he urged, his deep voice cutting through the growing chaos, "We're all in this together."

But as more people joined in, it became clear that the crowd's collective exhaustion and stress were turning this simple disagreement into a volatile situation. A flap near the main entrance of the tent moved and a handful of soldiers emerged, their uniformed presence immediately drawing attention.

"Enough!" bellowed the sergeant in charge, her voice amplified by a portable megaphone. "Step back and return to your positions in line. Now!"

Soldiers, their faces masked by the seriousness of their duty, moved through the crowd, ensuring people heeded the order. One, noticing the elderly woman on the ground, signaled for a medic.

Daphne, her heart racing, clutched at Jocelyn's arm.

Jocelyn gave her a reassuring pat. "They're here to help. It'll be okay."

Samuel, looking equally concerned but striving to

remain composed, added, "They're just trying to keep things in order. Everyone's on edge."

Despite the assurances, the scene only deepened Daphne's anxieties. There weren't enough FEMA staff to keep things in order. It was not only filthy and overrun, but dangerous, too. She knew in her gut they wouldn't be able to last long in this disarray.

Once it was finally their turn to check in at the tent, Daphne almost gasped. The woman behind the table looked as bad as Daphne felt. Her greasy hair was pulled up into a haphazard bun. Dirt was caked under her fingernails and some weird, unidentifiable gray grime was smeared across the bottom of her chin. Sweat stains ringed her armpits.

With a vacant expression, she took their names. Daphne hated to add to the pressure the woman was under, but she needed information. "I'm sorry, but can you tell me any details about inside? Are there showers? Changes of clothes?"

The woman began to recite the details as if she were a robot, not a living person. "Once you're past the main tent, we have stations set up. Showers are in short supply and first come, first served. Clothes are in the tent third from the right. As for sizes, I have no idea. You'll have to just pick through whatever's left."

Daphne swallowed. "And places to sleep?"

"Honestly, I don't know ma'am." She almost sagged. "Last I heard, we're at capacity."

"Well is there any place we can rest at least?"

The woman brought her hands up to clutch the top

of her head. "You're overwhelming me with questions I can't answer. As far as I know, we're out of cots, and pillows, so don't bother asking. People are packing in like sardines, not listening to instructions, stealing from each other." She trailed off, shaking her head.

Daphne glanced down at her feet blackened from her journey. She knew cuts criss-crossed her heels and one of the toenails on her left foot was cracked and bloody. She needed not just a shower, but a long soak and medical attention. If there were no showers, no shoes, not even a single place to sit...

The woman looked past her, trying to beckon the next person behind Daphne to come forward in line.

Daphne teared up and let a small cry escape her lips.

The woman glanced back and her features softened. She rested her hand on the table in front of her. "Look, I'm really sorry. I've been told to put the injured, old, and children first. Everyone else might just have to rough it outside, or on their own elsewhere. There's no one keeping you here. If you can find better shelter or conditions elsewhere, I'd definitely suggest it."

Daphne glanced up. While they'd inched up the line, the skies had darkened with clouds. The possibility of more rain was high. She couldn't imagine sleeping outside as rain pelted her. It would be miserable.

She tried one last desperate attempt with the woman. "I'm looking for my family. Is there any way I might check the lists to see if they've been through here?"

The woman adamantly shook her head, although her features were apologetic. "I'm sorry, no. There are too many. I have no idea when those lists will be consolidated. Currently, there is no way for me to check. I don't even have access to all the lists."

Daphne felt Samuel's hand go to her shoulder and he gave it a tender squeeze of solidarity. A single tear slid down Daphne's cheek.

The woman pointed behind her. "Inside, there's temporary fencing set up. Some survivors have started writing names on scraps of paper and attaching them to the fence. Some are leaving pictures. If you want to try and see if you find your family's names on there, go for it."

Daphne offered as polite a smile as she could muster and gave the woman her thanks. Samuel, still with his hand on Daphne's shoulder, led her and Jocelyn past the registration and inside.

She knew she should head straight to the clothes and then the showers, but as she turned to her left, the sight stole her breath. A fence spanned the whole length of the camp, hundreds of feet long. A good portion was blanketed with scraps of paper and pictures, names and faces of the missing. There had to be thousands. Tens of thousands. All missing. All unaccounted for.

She stumbled backward, her fingers brushing across her lips. Even if Clint and Mika had come here, even if they'd written her name on a scrap of paper with directions of where to go and how to reach them, how was she ever going to find it?

Daphne's eyes methodically scanned each part of the fence, lingering on every name, tracing the contours of every faded and torn photograph, and absorbing the raw emotion of every hastily scribbled note. With every step, she hoped to catch a glimpse of Mika or Clint's handwriting, a simple mark that would indicate they were out there, still holding fast to the bond they shared. But as she reached the end, the realization settled heavily: neither her name nor theirs were among the multitudes represented.

A hollow pang of disappointment stabbed at her chest. The memory of the FEMA worker's clipboard with their names written in block letters had been a beacon, a symbol that Clint and Mika were on her trail. But now? There was no sign of them in this crowded and chaotic space.

Daphne stood stock still, a lost silhouette amidst the

sea of desperation until a slight movement caught her attention. About ten feet away, another woman, her face etched with similar hope and dread, was searching intently, her fingers skimming each note and image pinned to the fence.

All at once, the woman froze. She reached out and gently tugged a piece of paper from its position. Daphne watched as the woman's knees buckled, her body crumpling to the ground. Tears flowed freely, but these were not borne out of despair; they were tears of profound relief. The woman clutched the paper to her chest, her sobs echoing with a mixture of joy and gratitude.

Daphne's heart twisted. On the one hand, genuine happiness surged inside her for the stranger. But on the other, the stark contrast of their situations weighed heavily on her heart. The juxtaposition of their experiences—the joy of one and the heartache of the other—amplified Daphne's own grief, emphasizing the void she felt at not finding any trace of her husband or daughter.

Dark thoughts began to cloud her mind. What if something terrible happened to Clint and Mika while they'd been searching for her? What if they'd been on another bus, one that suffered the same gruesome fate as hers? She quickly shoved the panoply of horrors down, but their shadows lingered, cold and unsettling. The idea that she alone seemed to dodge catastrophe time and again was both a blessing and a curse.

She turned away from the disappointment and headed to where Jocelyn and Samuel rested on a bench outside the shower facilities. Doubt gnawed at Daphne as she walked. Was she risking their safety for a potentially futile quest for a lost family? The "what-ifs" echoed incessantly and she cast her gaze about, searching for a diversion from her internal torment.

Everywhere she looked, she found reminders of her missteps. A little girl in dirty pajamas, thumb shoved between her lips. A father standing with his young son as tears streamed down his dirt-stained face. A harried FEMA employee rushing by with a box of latex gloves. If only she'd chosen differently, she'd be with Clint and Mika now, a unified family, surviving this disaster together.

Instead, she'd left them, and for what? Guilt infiltrated every fiber of her being. All this time they'd been apart, with her living her supposed "best life" in Bellevue, she'd been running away from hard work. Running away from her failures. She was the rift in the family fabric, and though she yearned to mend it, the chaos surrounding her underscored the challenge.

Her priorities had been so skewed. Her friends had become her surrogate family, sidelining those who mattered most. Sure, Clint had pulled away. But how hard had she worked to understand why?

Now, with the weight of their potential loss heavy on her heart, all fingers pointed back at her. As she neared the bench where Samuel and Jocelyn awaited, Daphne wrapped her arms around herself, trying to keep the tears at bay.

Jocelyn quickly rose, noticing Daphne's visible distress, and gently placed a hand on her shoulder. "Any clues?"

Without lifting her gaze, Daphne shook her head, haunted by the realization that there was no evidence of her family having passed through. "I've let them down." She shivered, a shadow of defeat hanging over her.

"Nonsense."

"But I did," Daphne lamented, letting her tears flow without restraint, her defenses shattered. "Mika was growing up and she didn't need me every second. Instead of finding a way to connect with her again, I left."

She snuffed back her tears. "Clint and I—" She struggled to find the right words. "We'd reached an impasse, but instead of confronting our issues, I left." She clung to Jocelyn as she sobbed.

"You mustn't shoulder all the blame," Jocelyn insisted. "You didn't just go out for a pack of cigarettes and never come back. You'd been drifting apart. It happens." Jocelyn gave her arm a squeeze. "It takes two to tango, you know."

On any other day, she would have agreed with her, but after pinning all her hope on finding her daughter here, on reuniting with her husband, on finally putting the pieces back together, it felt hollow and insincere.

"Let's find that clothing spot," Jocelyn suggested. "We're gross and nasty and you've got to be freezing."

Drying her tears, Daphne nodded. While Samuel stayed behind to rest on the bench, Daphne let Jocelyn lead her to the clothing area. She waited behind a family as disheveled as she felt, the mother in flood-ravaged jeans and a torn T-shirt. Once they reached the front of the line, a FEMA aide guided them to peruse the available selections, restricting them to just three items each.

Daphne began her search amidst the bins. A pair of gray sweatpants caught her attention; they seemed about her size. Holding them up, they reached just above her ankles. Not perfect, but certainly better than what she had on. Tucking them under her arm, her search continued.

Next, she stumbled upon a pair of bright pink flip-flops, boldly proclaiming "fun in the sun" on the soles. Daphne allowed herself a faint smile at the irony. A bin of T-shirts held plenty, all too big, but still better than what she had. She collected her three things and waited for Jocelyn to finish.

Soon after, they were guided to the makeshift showers. The water was brisk and the soap harsh, but the simple act of scrubbing away the grime invigorated her. Gone were the crusted lines of flood dirt and the black coating across her feet. She pulled on the fresh clothes and flip flops and threw her ruined blouse and pants into the nearest trash can.

It was such a small act, but it loomed large. She'd finally come out the other side of the disaster. Alone, but hopefully not forever.

She stood beside the exit, waiting for Jocelyn. The

rumble of a massive tractor trailer caught her off guard. Squinting past the fence, she tried to make sense of the flurry of activity surrounding it.

Soldiers in National Guard uniform hurried to open a gate in the fence before heading to the cab. Daphne tensed up, uncertainty gripping her, as they yanked open the driver's door.

CHAPTER TWENTY
CLINT

They drove on in silence for a long while as John navigated the quiet, smaller roads. But tensions were still high, and much of the carefree energy from the campground had long since vanished.

Underlying worry rippled through John's eyes every time he turned in his wife's direction and offered her a gentle smile. Michael stared out the window, posture rigid. It was clear to Clint that this family had never endured a traumatic experience like the hold up on the highway.

In the backseat, Madison clung tightly to Mika. She'd abandoned their card game and had resorted to burrowing her head in the crook of Mika's arm. His daughter tenderly stroked the little girl's hair.

Susan twisted, her gaze roaming across her family. "Everybody holding up okay?"

Michael gave her a curt nod.

She sighed, turned back around, and stared out the window.

Although no roving bands of refugees or enterprising thieves blocked their path, the smaller roads took concentration. More than once, John made a wrong turn and backtracked a few miles. As another intersection came into view, John's eyes lifted to the rearview mirror.

"Just keep following this route east," Clint offered. "It's your best bet."

John's chin tipped upward in an obliging nod before setting his eyes back on the road. No one said much else.

After about an hour, they came to a small intersection with one blinking yellow light. A small convenience store and gas station hugged the far corner. A *Stop-N-Go* sign hung slightly askew above the single-story building. Faded brown shingles and weathered, white wood siding covered the rest, all in desperate need of a pressure wash.

Another, taller sign usually sporting gas prices stood empty on the curb, but a handwritten sign tacked to the post proclaimed *we have gas!* in huge black magic marker letters.

John made eye contact with Clint again through the mirror. "We're not far from our place. Maybe thirty miles."

"You've been here before?"

John nodded. "We've camped nearby. I remember the building."

"How's the tank looking?"

"About half left." John eased into the gas station. "Shouldn't we—"

"Uh...Dad?" Michael sat up and squirmed in his seat. He licked his lips and nudged his chin toward the front of the store.

Clint followed Michael's nod before sucking in a sharp breath. A man's legs sprawled halfway out the door; the front half of his body still concealed inside. A pool of blood spread around his hips.

Without a word, Clint spun in his seat and made eye contact with Mika. She pulled Maddie close, all of a sudden fascinated by the little girl's rainbow sneakers.

"Should we help him?" Susan gasped; her eyes narrowed in on the body.

John's face drained pale. "It doesn't look like there's any help left to give."

"Best to keep going." Clint waved them on.

They pulled out of the parking lot and kept driving in silence. True to John's word, about forty-five minutes later, they pulled into the driveway of a squat brick ranch with a manicured lawn and a green front door. Before Clint even exited the vehicle, a neighbor lumbered across the road. He met John and Susan in the driveway.

"You're back!" He reached out and pumped John's hand in greeting one too many times. "Thought you might have run into trouble."

Clint climbed out through the opening in the rear of the minivan and the neighbor's eyes widened. Mika followed a moment later, with Maddie holding onto her hand.

The little girl stretched and yawned. "That took *forever*." She let go of Mika and ambled over to her mother. Susan rested her hand on her daughter's shoulder.

"You all okay?" The neighbor's gaze lingered on Clint.

John nodded, his whole body slumped with exhaustion and strain. He introduced Clint and Mika and the neighbor visibly relaxed.

"So you've been there? To the coast?"

"The Strait. And the east side of Seattle."

"Close enough." The neighbor glanced at Mika. "Is it as bad as the TV is making it out to be?"

"Worse." Clint filled him in on their saga, explaining how the tsunami wrecked Port Angeles and so much of the coastline of the area, and how the quake destroyed city block after city block. "We're trying to reach the FEMA shelter, the one here in Ellensburg. My wife might be there."

The neighbor nodded. "It's huge. Right on the edge of town." He turned to John. "You still have that map in your car?"

John strode over to the van and rummaged through the center console before coming back with a folded map of town. He handed it over and the neighbor opened it, refolding it to a manageable square.

"We're here." He pointed to an intersection amid what Clint guessed were a clump of residential streets. "The city really gets going over here." His finger tracked a mile or so. "The facility is here. You can't miss it. Big white tents, chain link fencing all around. It's..." he trailed off.

"What?" Clint asked.

"It's awful, to tell the truth. Way more people than anyone anticipated. They've spilled out into town, taken over all the hotels and short-term rentals. Clogged the stores, ran the restaurants out of food. There've been a fair number of fights. Shootings, too."

"Whoa." Michael stepped back, his face set in disbelief. He clutched the back of his head and glanced at his father. "We've missed a lot."

Susan shifted her weight uncomfortably, her eyes panning between her son and husband. "Maybe we should have stayed where we were at the campsite."

"We didn't have cell service back at the campground." John's face furrowed into a frown. "But that was normal. We didn't know."

"Reception's been spotty and data's been slow with all the added people. But—" the neighbor pulled out his phone— "it's all over social media. Look." He scrolled photo after photo of a massive facility with armed soldiers surrounded by a sea of refugees. In all the photos, people looked tired, frustrated, and dirty.

"May I?" Clint reached for the phone.

"Sure." The neighbor shrugged and handed it over.

Clint's eyes burned as he scrolled through picture after picture of flooded roads, landslides, and roads split in half with hollowed, dark holes left in their wake. People waving towels on top of buildings, waiting for rescue. Busted out windows of shops and grocery stores. Standoffs in the street with people wielding weapons. National Guard vehicles lined up in rows. Part of him hoped he'd see Daphne's face among the masses, but she was nowhere.

Dazed, Clint handed the phone back to the man.

"We hear gunshots every night." The neighbor looked at John and rubbed his hand down his arm. "It's probably best if you put the van in the garage. Don't leave your lights on at night, either."

John tilted his head. "Why?"

The neighbor shook his head and shoved his hands into his pockets. "At night, it's best to try and make it look like nobody's home."

"What about the National Guard?" Clint asked.

"We've seen a few. But not enough, and when they do filter through, it doesn't do much good. There's no structure or order."

Clint nodded. "There aren't enough of them, from our experience."

The neighbor smiled again at John and Susan. "Well, glad to have you back."

They made a bit more small talk before he headed back to his house across the street. John and Susan exchanged a daunted look before turning to the van. With everyone's help, they unloaded. John took his neighbor's advice and pulled the vehicle into the garage. Once inside, John stared at Clint and Mika for a long moment, as if he wasn't sure what to do.

"We can get out of your hair," Clint offered. "I just need a few minutes to gear up."

"Hon, they probably need showers and a change of clothes, don't you think?" Susan spoke up from the kitchen where she unloaded the remaining shelf-stable food back into the cabinets.

"Uh, yeah, I guess?" John rubbed the back of his head with an apologetic shrug.

"You can borrow something from my closet, Mika. And Clint, I can get you some spare clothes from John's dresser."

"That's very kind of you." Clint glanced again at John. He had the distinct impression the man was ready for them to leave. "But we don't need to take any more of your time."

Susan appeared in the doorway a moment later, wiping her hands on a dishtowel. "Nonsense. You two have been through so much. If the FEMA facility is as bad as it sounds, then there might not be anything available there. You don't want to be dirty and covered in sweat for days when you don't have to."

Clint turned to Mika. Her lips moved, but she couldn't quite manage a smile. "What is it?"

"Don't you think we should keep going? Looking for Mom, I mean? If the place is really that crazy—"

Clint reached out and gave his daughter's shoulder a squeeze. "We will. But Susan's right. If it's chaos there, it would be better to clean up here, repack, and hit the road in an hour. It's only a few miles from here. We'll be there before dark."

Mika glanced down at her clothes and wrinkled her nose. "I am pretty gross."

"Same." Clint lifted his head and smiled at Susan. "If you're sure you don't mind."

"Of course not." Susan led Mika to her bedroom to find a change of clothes before showing her the bathroom.

As soon as she returned, Clint took the opportunity to talk to Susan and John alone. "If things are as bad as your neighbor let on, you all need to be careful."

"About what?"

"Looters. Even if they don't come by the house, parking lots might be risky for a while. Clogged roads, too." He paused. "It might not go as easily as the last time."

John rubbed his fingers across his jawline. "So, you're saying we're not even safe in our own town?"

Clint paused before answering, choosing his words carefully. "I'm saying that things could get worse before they get better, and it's always good to be prepared."

"We *do* have some canned food and cases of water in the garage." Susan looked at John. "We should be able to last a little while on that without going to the store."

"Good." Clint nodded in encouragement. "That's better than nothing. And your neighbor seemed like a decent man. You can help each other."

"He's great," John admitted.

"But if things get really bad, we can always go to my parents." Susan turned to Clint. "They live in Montana."

The door to the bathroom opened, a plume of steam rising out into the hallway. The sound of the fan hummed from inside. Mika emerged, clad in a maroon sweatshirt and black joggers borrowed from Susan. Her wet hair hung down her back, dampening the sweatshirt in splotchy patches.

She gave Susan a shy smile, standing tall and lanky in the hallway, a little awkward in a stranger's home. "Thanks again for letting me borrow your clothes."

"Of course, honey." Susan offered her a tender, maternal smile.

Clint took his shower next, dressed quickly, and everyone said goodbye at the door. There were a few tears from Maddie, but Mika tickled them away. John thanked Clint for handling the gun-altercation in the traffic jam.

For a moment, John offered to drive them to the FEMA facility, but Clint waved him off. The family had done enough already. He didn't want to put them in another potentially dangerous situation. Hopefully within the day, they would find her mother.

CHAPTER TWENTY-ONE
MIKA

"How you holding up?" Mika's dad slipped his hands beneath his backpack straps and glanced over at her.

They'd been walking for about half an hour. Mika knew she was slow, but she'd managed to carry her own backpack this far. Maybe the food, and the warmth of the family they'd just left had done more for her than she'd thought. "Good, actually." She hesitated. "Better, at least."

"You let me know when you need a break."

She glanced up the road. "How much longer, do you think?"

"Another mile, maybe two."

Mika lifted her head toward the sky. The cloud cover kept the sun at bay and although she'd shed the sweatshirt, she wasn't overheated. So far, the walk had been uneventful, almost pleasant. But she couldn't shake the exhaustion that lingered in her limbs or the occasional dizzy spell that forced her to palm the nearest tree.

She clenched and unclenched her left hand. It was numb most of the time, but she thought maybe it was getting better. When this was all over, she would explain her symptoms to her parents and they would take her to a doctor. She'd be checked out and everything would be fine. She just needed to keep it together until then.

"What do you think Mom is doing right now, if she's at this FEMA place?" She hiked her backpack a bit higher on her back.

"She's probably combing every tent for a hot meal or a hot shower."

Mika laughed. "She's probably going nuts with the lack of hygiene."

"Even *I* am at this point," her dad admitted. "But the shower was great."

Mika sighed and tried to concentrate on the walk, but her mind kept straying. Ever since the shock, she'd had a hard time paying attention. Harder than she wanted to admit. She glanced up ahead. The residential area began to thin at the next block, changing into something more commercial. What looked like a strip mall sat on one corner with a park across the street.

Worry nudged her and she turned to her dad. "What if we run into more trouble?"

He squinted, assessing the road. "I don't see anyone. Besides, at least this time we're prepared." He patted the rifle slung across his shoulder.

Mika exhaled roughly. She wanted to believe him, but after everything they'd seen, she wasn't sure. "What if we get there and Mom isn't there? What if she never made it?"

Her dad stopped walking. "No sense in dwelling on all these possibilities, kiddo. They'll drive you crazy."

"Aren't you the one who's always telling me to be prepared?"

"There's a difference between being prepared and being anxious for no reason." He turned back to the road and began walking again. "At the moment, we're well fed, as well rested as we've been the past week. We're clean and we've got at least a first line of defense with this rifle. At this point, it's okay to hope for the best."

"And if it doesn't pan out?"

"Then we'll figure it out. But I'm not going anywhere. You can count on me."

Mika smiled down at the ground. "I know, Dad."

They slipped into silence, Mika attempting to shove the parade of horribles out of her mind, as her dad kept his eye on the road. Traffic picked up as they left the residential area behind, and Mika and Clint stuck to the sidewalk. Most of the shops in the strip mall were closed, though, and the park across the street seemed quiet.

Maybe her father was right; worrying about the future wasn't productive right now. But Mika couldn't help it. She could shove thoughts of her mom still missing and injured out of her mind, but then images of the Strait lapping against the concrete where their house used to be crowded in. She chewed on her lip for a long moment before speaking up again.

"Once we find Mom, and we're all okay, what are we going to do?"

Her father's face scrunched. "About what?"

"We don't exactly have a place to live, you know."

Her father's face relaxed into a smile. "Here I thought you were going to drop a family bomb on me. Housing is easy. We'll find another one."

"In Port Angeles? You probably don't even have a job anymore."

Her father shrugged. "Maybe. Maybe not."

Mika thought about it a long moment, the city around them disappearing into the background as her brain worked overtime. "Won't it take a long time to rebuild?"

"Years, I'm guessing. Most of Seattle will have to be torn down. Rebuilt. Same with all the coastal towns that suffered catastrophic damage."

"Can we wait that long?"

Her father shrugged. "We don't have to. I can be a facilities manager anywhere. We don't have to move back to Port Angeles. We could go somewhere new."

"What about Mom?"

"What about her?" Her father kept his eyes on the road, but Mika caught the hesitation in his voice.

"Do you think she'll want to go with us if we move?"

Her father was quiet as he thought it over. "Maybe. I don't really know what your mother will be willing to do now."

Mika frowned. She'd heard bits and pieces from her mother, explaining her decision to leave Port Angeles and strike out on her own in Bellevue, but she'd never really talked to her dad about it. He'd always shut down before, become closed and guarded. She'd always dropped it. She turned to him and waited until she caught his eye. "Why did Mom leave?"

His mouth fell open and his jaw worked back and forth.

"The real reason, Dad. Not some made up nonsense you think will make me feel better."

A rueful smile spread across her father's face and he shook his head. "You've grown up a lot this past week, you know?"

She raised an eyebrow.

He held up his hands. "Okay." He was quiet as he came up with the right words. "The truth is, we grew complacent. *I* grew complacent. When your mom and I met, we'd come from different places, and met in the middle. She'd always wanted to go back to the big city, live in the heart of it all. But when you came along, and I got the job in Port Angeles—"

"She compromised."

He nodded. "I fell in love with the place. The small town feel, how everyone knows your name. But Daphne..." He lifted his ball cap and ran a hand over his hair. "Daphne didn't. I thought she was okay with staying, or at least that's what I told myself. But deep down, I knew she wasn't."

"So why didn't we move?"

He let out a long, slow sigh. "Every time she brought it up, I basically shut it down. I just thought eventually she'd come to see it my way. I was happy at my job, you were happy at school, it was working. But—"

"Mom wasn't happy."

"Not really. I should have been willing to try something new. To figure out a way we could all be happy, at least most of the time."

"Why didn't you?"

Her father didn't answer. He tucked his head and stared down at the concrete beneath their feet for so long, Mika thought he wouldn't. But at last, he lifted his head. "To be honest, I don't really know."

They slipped into silence, then, Mika attempting to understand why her parents grew apart, and her dad thinking over everything they'd just discussed. As they passed into another residential area, he spoke again. "What about Boise?"

Mika gave him a puzzled glance. "What about it?"

"You remember that family trip we took out there?"

"Yeah? I think so. We went to those huge waterfalls, right?"

"Yep. Shoshone Falls, the Niagara Falls of the West." He used a fake announcer voice and Mika laughed. "It's only a few hours from here."

Mika stopped walking. "Wait. Are you saying you want to move there?"

"I'm not saying it one way or another. I'm just adding it to the list of potential places we could start over."

Mika's mind wandered over the possibilities. A fresh start could be a positive thing. A clean slate. Something to help them all move on from everything they'd lost. "Boise's big, right?"

"Not as big as Seattle, but bigger than Port Angeles. Somewhere in the middle."

"A compromise."

"But it still has enough nature around to satisfy the two of us."

"And no ocean. A definite plus."

Her dad laughed. "Agreed."

A trickle of excitement and hope mixed together in Mika's chest and she savored it. Maybe after this ordeal, her family would reunite, all in one place. They could start over somewhere new, together.

With her imagination running wild over the possibilities, the rest of the walk passed quickly. She failed to notice they were approaching the FEMA facility until her dad reached out and took her by the elbow.

"What?" She glanced around, startled.

"We should slow down." He nodded up ahead.

Mika blinked in disbelief. There had to be hundreds of people. They milled about on the street, blocking the road, clogging up traffic. Men in National Guard uniforms stood on the sidewalks, guns ready.

Her father eased up beside a tree and slipped the rifle and pack off his shoulders.

"What are you doing?"

Without answering, he checked the safety on the rifle and shoved it between the shoulder straps, managing to lift both it and the pack onto his back. Now the long gun was partially concealed behind him. He still kept one hand on the strap, but at first glance, he appeared unarmed.

Mika shuddered. If it wasn't safe to walk around with the rifle exposed, was it even safe to enter the facility?

Her father nodded toward the crowd. "We need to be careful. First sign of trouble, we walk away and regroup."

"But Mom—"

He held up a hand. "We'll find her. But we need to be smart."

Mika nodded, all the warm, fuzzy feelings over a potential family reunion displaced by a growing sense of dread. Her father reached out and took her hand, squeezing so tight it hurt, and they resumed their trek toward the mass of bodies milling about. Whatever this place had become, it wasn't welcoming. Mika hoped if her mother was inside, that she was somewhere safe.

CHAPTER TWENTY-TWO
DAPHNE

The thrum of the truck's idling engine vibrated through the encampment. After a moment, it shut off and the soldiers escorted the driver down from the cab and slammed the door.

"What do you think's inside?" Jocelyn queried, eyes narrowing in speculation.

"Supplies, we can hope. Food. Water." A note of guarded optimism carried in Samuel's voice.

People both inside and outside the facility seemed to notice the truck as well. A shout rang out from somewhere behind Daphne and fellow refugees began to stream past their little trio. A woman almost caught Daphne with an elbow, but she didn't apologize or even break stride.

A man jostled Samuel and he shifted closer to the women. "Whatever it is, everybody seems to want a piece of it."

"So shouldn't we?"

Daphne glanced at Jocelyn. "You really want to get caught up in all that?" As they watched, more and more people from outside the fence began to crowd the rear of the trailer. It reminded Daphne of images of relief aid dropped by the UN in war torn areas. She wrapped a protective arm around her middle. "I think we should wait it out."

"But that woman at check-in said there wasn't enough food or water. Shouldn't we head up there, try to grab some?" Jocelyn swayed back and forth, willing the little group to edge closer to the trailer.

"We don't know that for a fact. We don't even know what's inside that thing." Daphne turned to Samuel for support. "Maybe we should hang back, for safety."

As Samuel opened his mouth, a soldier brushed past them, followed quickly by a man wearing a yellow vest. The pair pushed through the crowd, the soldier doing his best to forge a trail. As soon as he cleared a path, the gap closed behind them, people surging forward, pressing closer and closer together.

Anticipation clogged the air as all the trampling feet lifted dust in small clouds all around them.

"Everyone, please step back!" A distorted voice shouted from somewhere near the truck. A large, rolling gate in the fence rolled back and the people inside the facility all pressed forward in a rush.

After a moment, the man who'd passed them in the yellow vest climbed onto the rear bumper of the truck in front of the rolling door. He held a megaphone to his lips. "Please, everyone remain calm!"

Jocelyn snorted beside her. "A little late for that."

The more the man talked, the more people ignored him, pressing ever closer to the truck. Daphne guessed most people believed he wouldn't be there if there wasn't something good inside. A throng of people emerged from the area just behind her and within moments, their little trio was caught up. Daphne struggled to keep the dollar flip flops on her feet, clutching them with her toes as she was jostled toward the truck.

They'd gone from watching on the sidelines to being swept up in the melee in a matter of seconds. Daphne forced down a wave of panic. As long as she stayed on her feet, with her wits about her, she'd be fine. But no sooner had the thought formed in her mind, when Jocelyn cried out.

Daphne strained to reach her, gripping the hairdresser's hand in hers and pulling her back. "Stay with me!" She shouted over the crowd noise, but she wasn't sure Jocelyn even heard.

A sea of people flooded the area, all pressing toward the truck, closer and closer together. If there had been any guardsmen near the gate, they were severely outnumbered and didn't seem to be doing anything about the crowd. From her vantage point, Daphne only caught glimpses here and there of the truck and the ground.

She turned, searching for Samuel. Another burst of panic shot through her, but she found him a few people back, also being propelled forward by the crowd. She twisted again to the front.

Someone elbowed her in the side. Jocelyn pressed close and almost stepped on her toes. Another woman beside her screamed as she fell to her knees. Daphne swallowed hard.

Hands and elbows shoved against her, pushing her into Jocelyn. Panicked faces surged around her. Anguished pleas and tense shouts rang out. Daphne's heart raced, thudding heavily in her chest, matching the chaotic rhythm of the throng. Each gasp for air felt like a battle, the surrounding pressure stifling her breath.

An unexpected push from behind made her stumble forward, her feet tangling with Jocelyn's. She tightened her grip on the other woman's hand, her fingers white with strain, as Jocelyn's body tensed and swayed with her. Daphne felt like she was back in the flood water as the current dragged her down.

Her eyes darted around, scanning the frenzied crowd. She tried to shout to Jocelyn, to confirm her presence by her side, but her voice was swallowed by the cries and yells around them, lost in the chaos.

The man at the truck tried the megaphone again, but it was no use. Daphne couldn't hear over the shouts all around her. Her mind whirred as the pressure around them escalated. The pushing intensified and desperation grew more palpable, every shove a possible injury. Up ahead, someone attempted to climb onto the back of the truck, but was pulled back by an unseen hand.

A child's cry cut through the noise as his mother attempted to lift him from the ground. He was caught in a sea of adults, all jostling against him. Tears streamed down his face as a man barreled into him, desperate to reach the trailer.

A woman beside Daphne, with frenzied eyes and cheeks stained with tears, clutched the hands of two small children, trying to shield them from the onslaught of bodies, her voice a thin shriek amidst the tumult as she pleaded for space. Nearby, a tall man, his face twisted in a mask of determination and frustration, used his height to scan the surroundings, his arms pushing and shoving, creating a temporary cocoon around him in his quest to move forward.

In a fleeting moment, Daphne lost grip on Jocelyn's hand. She was there, and then she was gone. Turning swiftly, she found her on the ground, being crushed by a family desperately trying to reach the front. Jocelyn gasped, her eyes wide, hands clawing at the dirt. She tried to scream, but only a strangled sound emerged.

"Joce!" Daphne, her heart pounding, knelt beside her friend, pulling at Jocelyn's arm, but she was pinned.

"Get off her!" Daphne yelled, shoving a man in the back of the leg. "Move!"

The man didn't budge. Anger swelled in Daphne and she surged forward, leading with her shoulder. She knocked the man clear to the ground, his body flailing forward and into several others. Falling half on top of him, Daphne clawed her way back across his legs as she reached for her friend.

Her fingers brushed over Jocelyn's braids as she searched for her arm, but she wasn't fast enough.

Someone stumbled over her as she bent forward, still half on the ground. A foot collided with her ribs. She inhaled sharply and the world around her blurred. Her breath was caught in her throat. The overpowering stench of sweat, dirt, and urine filled her senses. Daphne gagged and her vision dimmed.

Someone trudged into her, sending her rolling away from Jocelyn. She cried out, but the sound was carried away by the crowd. Her cheek grazed a boot and she reached for her face, fingertips coming away bloody.

The sound of a truck gate rolling up cut through the din and within seconds, the crush of bodies morphed into a hive of panic. Feet pounded beside her and people crushed in on all sides. Daphne had to stand or she'd be trampled.

With a deep breath that finally reached her lungs, Daphne managed to get her legs underneath her. She surged upright, windmilling her arms to keep the crush of bodies at bay.

It worked, barely. She managed to stand, both flip flops still on her feet. But pain spread across her ribs where someone had landed an inadvertent blow and her cheek stung from the fresh cut.

"Water! They have water!" A voice beside her called out and Daphne turned toward the truck.

She squinted and rose up on her toes to try and see. Ahead, hundreds of arms reached toward the sky, hands out and open. Sure enough, bottles of water flew from the truck, one after another into the crowd. They had been right. The truck was full of supplies.

But Daphne would have traded all the water in the world to not be there, almost trampled to death, in that moment. She scanned the crowd for any sign of her friends and came up empty.

Bryce Gibbs stood on the edge of the trailer bumper, sweat slicking his grip on the useless megaphone. Four days ago, he'd been sitting in a windowless classroom in the basement of a FEMA facility in Southern California, receiving a crash course in disaster relief.

Fresh out of college, Bryce was two months away from starting his job in a high school in inner city LA, a Teach for America new recruit. But rent in Los Angeles bordered on the criminal and he needed as much extra cash as he could put his hands on before August.

So when FEMA offered to pay a premium for emergency relief workers during the crisis, he hopped in his Honda Civic hatchback and drove to the nearest facility to sign up. Here he was, less than a week later, woefully unprepared for the sight in front of him.

No one told him the relief facility he'd been assigned was a dirty tent on the edge of a small town with nowhere near enough staff and an overwhelming influx of refugees. No one told him the people showing up would be hungry, exhausted, and reeking of filth and decay. He sucked in a breath and almost gagged on the smell.

Below him, a teeming mass of humanity ebbed and flowed, men hurling insults at his feet, women crying as they cradled small children in their arms. He'd tried to get them to listen. Tried to make an orderly line. But it was useless.

The National Guardsman who'd helped him snake through the crowd to the truck was nowhere to be seen. Granted, he hadn't been the friendliest to the soldier, but staring out at the frenzied horde below him, he was beginning to rethink his opinion on firearms. With a deep breath he steeled himself. He'd just open the door and start handing out the supplies. What was the worst that could happen?

Before he even bent toward the latch, a beefy brick of a man, all chest and biceps, hauled himself up. Bryce recoiled in horror. Was he standing on someone's back? Was he eight feet tall?

The man reached thick, meaty fingers toward the latch. Bryce swallowed. Should he try to stop him? Could he? He glanced at the megaphone still in his hand. He could use it as a weapon, he supposed, but that would only make the veritable giant enraged.

In the end, Bryce did nothing, almost stepping out of the way as the man hoisted the latch open and shoved the rolling door of the trailer open. The second the door slammed against the stop, a wail rose from the crowd and everyone pressed forward, rushing the truck like it was Black Friday and there was only one flat screen TV left.

Stunned, Bryce staggered into the open trailer. The megaphone slipped through his fingers and bounced against the metal floor. The clang of metal-on-metal shook Bryce into action and he bent to retrieve it. He brought it to his lips and clicked the button as he turned toward the crowd.

"Alright. We've got water and food inside. Plenty for everyone, But this needs to be orderly. We're going to form a line."

"The hell we are." The man who'd thrown open the door hauled himself inside and rose to his full height. At least a foot taller than Bryce and seventy-five pounds heavier, he dwarfed the recent college graduate.

Without another word, the man turned toward the shrink-wrapped pallet of water bottles and tore into it, ripping the wrap to shreds.

Bryce stepped forward. "What are you doing? That's FEMA property. Rules are that only—"

The man whirled around to face Bryce. "What rules?" He motioned toward the crowd. "The same rules that claimed we'd have a warning of any mega quake? The same rules that prevented emergency responders from reaching my neck of the woods until the water receded? The same rules that pinned us all in here like cattle with no food or water before kicking us out with a worthless voucher and a set of clothes from Goodwill?"

Bryce swallowed. He didn't know what to say. Maybe

if he reasoned with him... "We need to have a system for divvying out the supplies fairly."

"There's no fair involved in this, kid." The man turned back around and ripped the last of the plastic wrap away. He grabbed two water bottles in each hand and threw them over his shoulders and out into the crowd. Screams rose up as he threw more and more.

Bryce edged away from the opening as people in the crowd rushed forward, arms extended. A man in front fell from the crush of the crowd, his head hitting the metal bumper of the trailer. Blood spattered across the latch. Another man caught a water bottle, only to be punched hard in the side of the head. He disappeared into the mass of bodies.

Another man jumped into the trailer.

"You can't be up here!" Bryce waved his arms, tried to shout.

The man spun on an angry heel, face red, nostrils flaring. "What'd you say to me kid?"

Bryce took a step back, hands up.

"That's what I thought." The man turned around and joined the burly one who still ripped and tore at the water pallet, throwing bottles as fast as he could manage. Together, they were a force, bottles flying through the air so fast, the pallet would be empty in minutes.

When there was no more water they would move on to the food—boxes of granola bars and trail mix, mostly. When that was gone, what then? The crowd would erupt.

Bryce stared out at the sea of people. He needed back

up. He needed the National Guard. He brought the megaphone back to his mouth and clicked the button. "Hey! We need some help up here! Are there any guardsmen in the area? Help! We need help!"

A scurry of movement caught his eye, a flash of black and green. Bryce exhaled in relief. They would find a way through. Everything would be all right. He leaned back against the wall of the trailer and closed his eyes for a moment. But it was short lived. Something brushed across his legs and as he opened his eyes, he found two more men inside the truck, heading toward the food.

He scanned the crowd. The National Guard were working their way forward, but they were slow, trapped behind the sea of bodies. They would take too long. By the time they reached the truck, all the food and water would be gone.

Bryce took a deep breath. This was his job. This was what he'd signed up for. He stepped forward, easing in front of the two men at the food.

"No!" He stopped in front of the pallet, arms outstretched, palms flat in front of him. "You can't take this. We need to sort through it and form a line. Everyone will get their chance."

The first man reached out, ready to shove Bryce aside, when he widened his stance and his arms. "I said *no*."

For a moment, the man hesitated, but only for a moment. Behind him, the first interloper, the one with tree trunk thighs and a neck to match, lumbered over.

"He in the way?"

"Sure is."

The first man shook his head. "I'm done with this." In one swift movement, he reached for Bryce, grabbing him around the waist and hoisting him up like a sack of flour. Bryce screamed.

He tried to use the megaphone, clicking the button as he brought it up, but before he could call out, the man whipped him backward in a vicious arc and all of a sudden...

He was airborne. The floor of the trailer flew past him and he sailed, up and over heads and bodies and dirt. He was flying.

Mid-air, the sharp, unmistakable crack of a gunshot rang out. Followed by another and another. *Pop-pop-pop. Pop-pop-pop.* Over and over.

Time slowed. Everyone beneath him screamed. The crowd shifted away from the trailer and into each other, a circle dance like ants when their nest has been destroyed.

The ground rose up to meet Bryce and he slammed into it, face making first contact with the dirt. His teeth dug into his lip and the taste of copper and grit coated his tongue. He blinked and sweat and crud worked into his eye.

As he tried to press himself up to stand, feet scuffled over him. Someone's boot pinned Bryce's hand to the ground and he wailed in pain as something snapped in first one finger and then another. He fell back to the ground as another foot slammed down on the middle of his calf, pinning him to the earth.

A moment later, something heavy and thick fell on

top of him, the entire weight of it slamming into the middle of his back. Pain lanced his middle. Things snapped that shouldn't. He gasped.

At last, the weight eased and he tried to move his legs. A needling sensation traveled through his arms. He didn't move. Again, he tried to stand, but his muscles refused to respond. Tears bloomed in his eyes and streamed down his cheeks.

Another round of shots rang out, *pop-pop-pop*, and the melee became a stampede. The herd plowed across Bryce like wild horses on the loose, trampling over him without a single moment of hesitation. A water bottle landed beside his face, fresh water sloshing onto the ground and turning the dirt to mud. It shot up his nose and into his mouth. He couldn't breathe, couldn't move his arms to wipe the mud away. Couldn't roll over onto his side. He tried to cry out, but no sound escaped his lips.

A boot slammed into his temple. The world blurred. Something jabbed his chest, a sharp, brutal pain and suddenly the lack of oxygen, the lack of sight, the lack of bodily control ceased to matter. Bryce slipped into unconsciousness. His arms twitched. His legs spasmed. He let out one last dragging sigh, a mere bubble in the mud.

No one in the panicked crowd even noticed.

CHAPTER TWENTY-FOUR
MIKA

Pop-pop-pop. Mika froze on the edge of the crowd.

As soon as they'd spotted the semi-truck coming to a stop outside the chain link fencing, Mika and her father had picked up the pace, hoping to catch a glimpse of inside the facility without waiting in the massive, jumbled line outside.

A pair of soldiers had rolled a large gate in the middle of the fence back and took up guard positions while another two hurried to help the driver down. But as soon as the driver's boots hit the ground, everything kicked off. People from both inside and outside the fence swarmed the truck. Mika and her dad had been swept up, forced to either go with the flow of the crowd or push against it and risk separation.

Now they were trapped too close to the truck, wedged in tight amongst a sea of refugees all jostling for position. Her father grabbed her arm, looping his large one around hers, and attempted to keep them together.

Another round of gunshots. The crowd erupted around them, everyone turning this way and that, desire to reach the truck replaced with panic and a need to flee. A man slammed into Mika and his face contorted in rage.

"Move, you stupid girl!" He shoved her hard with both hands and a flash of pain sent her reeling backward. Her father managed to keep her upright by sheer force of will.

"Watch it!" Her father turned on the man, all anger and instinct.

The guy huffed and reeled his arm back, attempting to punch her father, but he missed wide. Her dad grabbed the man by the collar of his dirty shirt and hurled him out of their way.

"Come on! This way!" Her father shouted above the roar of panicked voices all around them, urging her away from the truck.

He tugged her close, attempting to break free from the stampede, but they merely shuffled ahead. Pinched by the crowd, they barely moved. Mika tried to breathe but the crush of bodies cut off her breath. People surrounded her on all sides, pushing, shoving, like tidal waves thrashing against her.

"Stay close," her dad yelled. "No matter what, do *not* let go of my hand!"

Mika tried her best, dodging another burly man using his chest and arms as battering rams. Her dad pulled her closer and she felt his lungs fill with air and the steady beating of his heart. She clutched him tight and inhaled, finally able to take a breath. A woman bumped into them both, tears streaming down her face as she clutched a gaggle of water bottles to her chest.

One fell, landing in a thud beside Mika's feet and she bent to pick it up. Blood whooshed through her ears and she stumbled, suddenly dizzy from the change in direction. Bodies moved all around her. Jeans, pants, skirts, bare knees and feet all jumbled like fruit in a blender.

Mika rose and a huge body slammed into her shoulder from the side. She stumbled and a stray elbow crashed into her temple, propelling her back. Her hand slipped away from her father and she clutched the side of her face as she doubled over, choking on her own spit. Nausea coiled through her body. The ground went wobbly and she struggled not to fall.

"Mika!" Her father screamed for her and Mika frowned. Wasn't he just here? She stared at her hands, confused. They were empty. She wasn't holding onto her dad or the water bottle. Only the thick, cloying air.

"Outta the way!" A man's voice funneled through her ears as hands shoved her in the shoulder. She stumbled again. The crowd swirled around her. Mika was lost in the storm of it, a pillar of indecision and frozen fright while everyone else swarmed.

Where was her dad? She managed to stand upright and scan the crowd, searching for his faded hat. But he was nowhere. She struggled to breathe. Panic closed her throat, tightened her chest, raced her heart. Someone shoved her in the side and she twisted around, barely staying upright.

As she turned, she caught a glimpse of a familiar woman with shoulder-length blonde hair. "Mom?" she called out, but her voice was swallowed in the surrounding din. She stepped forward, searching again for the woman, but everyone was in the way. She scanned the cluster of people around her, but nothing.

Had she made it up? Hallucinated the sight of her mother in this chaos? *No.* She shook her head and ground her fist into her palm. It was her mom. She was sure of it.

She turned around in a full circle, the chaos around her palpable. Everywhere she looked, people pushed and shoved, their faces masks of desperation and fear.

A young man, flushed and struggling, tried to shield a smaller woman from the jostling mass, but the force of the crowd pulled them in separate directions. His hand reached out, stretching towards her, but found only empty air. A frail elderly man stumbled and fell, his cane sliding away. Mika struggled to catch a glimpse of him, but a swarm of bodies swallowed all traces.

Anguished shouts and cries clamored all around her, punctuated by a child's sharp, terrified scream. Mika sucked in a breath, the air saturated with the scent of sweat and fear, and coughed. Tense energy radiated from every person, their panic almost a flavor on her tongue.

Her father was nowhere to be seen and the woman she'd glimpsed had disappeared into the crowd. She tried to move, but there were too many people to fight against. She didn't know where to run, where to look. How was she ever going to get out of there?

A current of terror rooted her to the spot and she

inhaled. If she didn't hold it together and find her parents, she wouldn't make it. She'd be trampled by the strangers all around her and her parents would have to scrape her body off the dirt.

No. She wasn't going to let that happen. As long as she kept her wits, she would make it out alive.

CHAPTER TWENTY-FIVE
DAPHNE

Daphne's eyes darted frantically from person to person, searching for any sign of Samuel or Jocelyn among the chaotic surge of bodies. They had vanished, leaving her isolated in this maelstrom of desperation and panic. All around her, voices were raised in terror and anger, the air dense with fear and hysteria.

Every ounce of her being was focused on maintaining her balance, on not being consumed by the tumultuous sea of humanity around her. Her muscles strained against the relentless pressure from every side, struggling to remain upright amidst the blows and shoves. The mass of frenzied individuals seemed to defy gravity, their elbows and arms colliding with her body, threatening to knock her down.

Her gaze flitted unceasingly over the horde surrounding her, scanning for any trace of her companions. How had they become so thoroughly separated in mere moments?

Wait—is that? Her attention snagged on a face in the crowd. Daphne squinted, disbelief wrestling with hope. It seemed impossible, but the similarity was undeniable.

Hair the color of sunlit honey so similar to her own. Lanky and tall, still awkward at sixteen. Exhaustion bent the girl's shoulders, each breath seeming to carry the weight of surrender. But it looked like her, at least from a distance.

For a heartbeat, Daphne grappled with the notion. Was her mind playing tricks, or had she really seen her daughter in this horrible, violent crowd? Doubt gnawed at her, but the image lodged in her mind. Daphne rose up on her tiptoes, but the swarm of bodies coalesced, hiding the girl from view. A desperate urgency propelled Daphne forward and she shouted at the closest body.

"Out of my way!" She shoved past the man, ignoring his shouts of anger and the push to her backside.

Where did she go? Daphne scanned the crowd, heartbeat reverberating in her ears with every dodge of a stranger, every dart to one side and then another.

Navigating through a thicket of bodies, she emerged and—*there!*

A jolt of recognition shocked Daphne and she brought her fingers to her lips. Her daughter stood stock still, fear sticking her in place, as the crush of the crowd hemmed her in. She looked so tired and fragile. *So young.*

"Mika!" Daphne's voice ripped from her as tears blurred her vision. She wiped them away and scanned the crowd for Clint. *Where is he? Why aren't they together?* Relief at seeing Mika was shadowed by the absence of her husband. Had something happened to him? Was Mika there all alone?

She called out again, straining to shout above the noise. "Mika!"

Her daughter turned her direction as a man pushed his way through. He jostled her and Mika stumbled, arms flailing wide. The sight kicked Daphne into gear and she surged forward, ignoring the pain of a knee to her hip, the jolt of a shoulder to her back, the cries of other women as she shoved them aside to reach her daughter. With every ounce of strength, she forged ahead, eyes locked on Mika.

"Mika!" She screamed again, voice hoarse from the strain and her daughter turned in her direction, eyes searching. At last, they found her and her daughter's face widened for a moment in shock before crumpling in relief. She rushed forward, propelled by instinct and love and they practically slammed into each other, both wrapping arms and squeezing tight. Her daughter quivered in her embrace, hot tears coating Daphne's cheek as she leaned close.

"Mom!"

The one word Daphne had longed to hear throughout this entire ordeal. The one word that kept her going despite the quake, the tsunami, the moment where she almost gave up.

"Mom." Her daughter sobbed against her shoulder and Daphne held her even tighter.

Daphne ran a hand down her daughter's hair. "It's okay, Mika. I'm here. I've got you."

As they stood fast together, the rumble of a helicopter

filled the air. Wind from the chopper's blades swept Daphne's hair into a tornado and she pulled back, holding her daughter at arm's length. "Are you okay?"

Mika nodded, tears coating her cheeks and darkening a shirt Daphne had never seen. Behind her, a commotion began along the fence line and Daphne sucked in a breath. More soldiers, wearing different uniforms from the National Guard, poured into the area.

Space opened up in the crowd and Daphne pulled Mika away from the fence and the truck and the soldiers infiltrating the chaos. She palmed her daughter's cheek. "I'm so grateful you're safe."

Tears streamed down Mika's cheeks. "I thought I'd lost you."

Daphne's grip tightened on Mika's shoulders, pulling her into another embrace. Her daughter was thinner than she remembered, with dark circles beneath her eyes and a bruise yellowing across her forehead. But she was alive and in her arms.

All at once she pulled back. "Your father—is he?"

A shadow crossed Mika's face as her eyes looked past Daphne. "We were separated... I don't—"

Daphne turned, pulse quickening at the sight of her husband navigating through the dispersing crowd, his eyes locked on hers. A mix of elation and nervousness fluttered within her, the reality of the impending reunion rooting her to the spot. A tumult of relief, hope, and anticipation swelled within her.

Clint closed the remaining distance with long, confident strides. He stared at her like he used to all those years ago when they first met. Daphne blinked back a fresh wave of emotion. Without a word, he extended his arms and Daphne stepped into his embrace. Her tears soaked into his shirt, all the regret and unfulfilled wishes washing away.

Mika squeezed in, and the three of them stood in the dirt of the wrecked FEMA facility while soldiers barked commands and restored order all around. Clint ran his fingers over her hair, pulling it back before planting a kiss on her forehead.

Despite everything, they were reunited. Her family was together and alive despite it all. They had survived, and they would recover, one careful step at a time. Gradually, the knot of fear within Daphne loosened, dissolving into relief and newfound strength.

Cherise McNeil was tired, but she was in the home stretch. With efforts shifted away from rescue to recovery and rebuilding, the high-pressure moments of her job had eased. She stared out at the rectangles of suited men on her laptop screen and managed a confident smile for the first time in over a week.

"Thanks to the 82nd Airborne, our facility at Ellensburg is safe and secure." She nodded at the Vice Chairman of the Joint Chiefs of Staff who'd begun to attend the calls in the Chairman's stead. "If they hadn't arrived when they did, things might have spiraled out of control completely."

"We heard there was loss of life, is that true?"

Cherise nodded. "One of our recent hires was trampled in the panic. It's tragic. His family has been notified."

"But you're sure the situation is contained?"

"Yes. One hundred percent," Cherise promised with

a nod and a moment of brief eye contact. "We're also about a day away from opening a second facility in Oregon. It should alleviate a significant amount of the pressure."

The Governor of Oregon spoke up. "Our National Guard is putting the finishing touches on the security plan for the Oregon processing facility and we're as confident as we can be that any violence will be kept to a minimum."

Cherise nodded in agreement. "Now that Sea-Tac is operational and flights have resumed, we've been able to bring in a significantly increased amount of supplies. Food, water, clothes, medical equipment. Everything is coming along nicely at this point."

Governor Peters chimed in. "We also have a fair amount of our public transportation running modified schedules throughout the affected region. City and county buses have been rerouted to transport anyone seeking assistance to either Ellensburg or a satellite facility."

Michael Urston, the head of FEMA, ran his finger down the agenda. "How are the numbers? Still seeing thousands of refugees arriving daily?"

Cherise shook her head. "Not nearly that many."

"Reason?"

"We've received reports of numerous people opting not to seek FEMA assistance, instead going directly to family members in other locations. Now that bus and air travel has resumed, we're seeing more flexibility on all fronts."

He scribbled something on his paper and Cherise exhaled a long, slow breath. Everything was finally coming together. The moving parts of the emergency response machine were slipping into place. It had been a nightmare, but the storm was clearing, and they were finally seeing some light in the darkness.

"The Army Corps of Engineers and Coast Guard have both been deployed to the hardest hit areas along the coast," Urston declared, moving on to the next order of business on the list. "They are helping with search and recovery and shoring up any dangerous areas along the coastline."

"Any chance of rescue at this point, or is it too late?" Peters asked, a hopeful note in his voice.

Urston managed a curt nod. "Of course, the possibility is always open."

Peters leaned back in his seat and the chair groaned in protest. Silence followed.

By transitioning to recovery, they all knew the truth: thousands, if not millions of people died in the disaster. Many would never be found. But that didn't stop the wheels of progress from moving. There were survivors—millions of them—and they needed running water and safe roads and a place to sleep at night.

Cherise cleared her throat. "Will the Army Corps of Engineers begin to assess the damaged pipelines soon? I know many are concerned about the potential natural disaster there."

The Vice Chairman leaned forward. "Yes, along with

repairing bridges and broken sea walls, the pipelines are a key priority."

"Power crews from eleven neighboring states are on their way to help repair damaged power lines in the areas hardest hit," Urston offered. "It might take some time, but power will eventually be restored to all areas. A lifeline is coming, at least."

"I'm confident we'll get there faster with the extra crews working around the clock," Peters agreed. "People were predicting a year or more without electricity, but I'm thinking months, if not weeks in a few areas."

Weeks was a bit too optimistic, but Cherise held her tongue. If Peters wanted to believe the best, then let him. He'd seen so much tragedy the last week, a little hope couldn't hurt.

At last, someone in the conference room at the White House spoke up. Cherise didn't recognize the man. "The Federal government has enacted a disaster assistance program. It will provide loans to individuals and small businesses on an emergency basis so they can rebuild."

"What are the terms of the loans?" Peters asked.

"The details are still being ironed out, but I believe there are many options, including total loan forgiveness to some who might qualify. It's run out of a combination of the Small Business Administration and partnerships with local banks."

The call continued, with the Governors of Washington and Oregon updating the White House on current predictions of total loss of life. Cherise tuned out the horror and concentrated on the positives. The water had receded to a level where scientists believed it might stay from now on. Anywhere from zero to three hundred feet of coastline was gone in various places, including whole streets in some areas, but it wasn't as bad as initially feared.

Millions of buildings were either heaps of rubble, or would need to be destroyed. But millions more withstood the quake and the flood. There would be problems with structural integrity and mold and countless other issues for years, but it could be worse.

It could always be worse.

Cherise was thankful for the support given by everyone from the youngest Private in the National Guard to the President this past week. She never wanted a single FEMA region to have to respond to a disaster of this magnitude, but Region Ten responded with all the grace and grit it could muster and then some. She was proud of her team and all they'd accomplished in such a short period of time.

The call began to wrap up, with the White House and several other participants leaving. After a moment, only the Governor of Washington remained. His face, now less blotchy and haggard, filled the screen.

Cherise smiled. "How are you holding up, Governor?"

Peters smiled. "I'm alive, thanks to you. Never did have a chance to thank you properly for the heads up."

She waved him off. "No need. Just doing my job."

"And a solid one it is. If the powers that be don't promote you after this, they're crazy."

Her grin spread so wide her cheeks hurt. "Maybe you could say that to someone who matters."

He whacked the table with his hand. "You betcha. Anything else I can do for you?"

"Get some sleep. In a bed."

Peters laughed. "You, too."

"If you need anything—"

"I know where to find you." Peters waved and a moment later, the screen went black.

Cherise slowly closed her laptop and her eyes. She'd lived a year in the past nine days, but overall, she was happy to have done her part. Rebuilding would be slow, painful even, but over time it would happen. All they needed was faith, perseverance and a great deal of hard work.

The silence post-chaos unsettled her, even now, almost twenty-four hours after finding her family. Daphne flinched at each noise, anticipating a skirmish or a volley of gunfire. No matter how hard she tried, she couldn't shake off the events of the day before. They'd managed to all huddle together inside the FEMA facility—her, Clint, and Mika—and catch a bit of sleep overnight.

But she still hadn't found Jocelyn or Samuel. All around them, the fresh influx of Army troops moved systematically, maintaining order and peace. But the sight unnerved her. The sooner they left this place behind, the better.

Daphne ran her hand over her daughter's hair as they sat at a bench, picking over the remains of a packaged breakfast. A tap landed softly on her shoulder and she turned to find Jocelyn standing behind her. Her long braids were mostly intact, apart from one area covered with a bandage on her scalp, and although her clothes were now dirty and torn in several places, she appeared okay.

Her smile warmed as soon as they made eye contact, the joy reaching her eyes as Daphne turned all the way around and wrapped her arms around the other woman. Tears stung in Daphne's eyes, blurring her vision. "I tried to help in the crowd, but—"

"I know." Jocelyn sniffled over Daphne's shoulder, her own shoulders shaking as she bit back a few sobs.

"We both made it, though," Daphne whispered, not trusting her voice. She pulled back after a long moment and introduced her to her family.

Jocelyn's smile widened as she waved at Mika. "You look so much alike, especially when you smile."

Daphne nodded in agreement. "So, have you thought about where you're going next?"

Jocelyn wiped a single tear off her cheek and took a deep breath, gazing at the cloud cover overhead. "I finally got through to my sister in Detroit. She's been frantic with worry. She's on her way. It'll take a bit to get here, but the FEMA folks gave me a voucher this morning for a hotel. They say it's nearby. They'll even give me a ride."

"That's incredible. I'm so relieved for you." Daphne gave her an earnest smile, meaning every word. But her eyes roamed beyond the other woman's shoulder, scanning the facility. Her eyebrows knit as she turned back to Jocelyn. "What about Samuel?"

"I saw him," Jocelyn nodded, her eyes brightening. "He's going to be okay. He got some treatment at the medic tent. He's—"

"Oh!" Daphne exclaimed, her hand instinctively reaching up to cup her mouth. "He's there!"

Striding toward them with only a hint of a limp, Samuel approached. He stopped in front of them and Daphne scooted forward, swinging her arms around him in a tight hug. He responded, wrapping his arms around her and squeezing back.

Daphne tilted her chin upward and grinned. "You made it out alive."

"A miracle, to be sure."

Samuel's eyes reached Clint behind her. Daphne stepped aside as the two men exchanged a firm handshake. Beside Samuel, a younger woman stood off to the side, a bit guarded and shy.

Samuel followed Daphne's gaze and smiled. "This is my daughter, Abby."

"Nice to meet you." They shook hands and Samuel beamed with pride.

"Abby drove all the way from Arizona to find me."

"Wow. That's dedication."

"She's quite the daughter."

Daphne turned toward Mika and scooped one arm around her waist, pulling her closer. "I've got one of those, too."

Mika blushed and flicked her gaze to her feet.

"We wouldn't have made it this far without your dad," Jocelyn explained to Abby. "If it weren't for him, I'd be knee deep in flood water or locked up because I finally snapped and took out some poor FEMA lady at a tent."

Daphne laughed. "She's right. If it weren't for your dad, we wouldn't be here."

Samuel's eyes brightened at the compliments and he rocked back a bit on his heels.

"Can we exchange contact information?" Jocelyn asked, her gaze shifting between them. She produced a piece of paper and a pen from a pocket. "They handed these out back at one of the tents."

"That'd be good." Daphne shared her number, a pang of sadness hitting her, realizing she had no permanent address to share. But dwelling on the uncertainties of the future was the last thing she wanted. The priority was they were alive, and they were together.

"It's comforting, seeing people find their families again," Jocelyn remarked, her voice trembling slightly. "But—"

"Let's not say goodbye," Daphne interjected, fighting back her emotions. "How about, see you later?" Parting with Jocelyn and Samuel—strangers turned friends—was inevitable, but it didn't make it any easier. "It sounds more hopeful."

"Alright." Jocelyn reached out again and pulled Daphne into a warm embrace. "Once I make it to Detroit, I'll call, make sure you're both doing okay." Jocelyn assured Daphne and Samuel, glancing at them both in turn.

"You better." Daphne gave her arm one last squeeze, and she watched as both Jocelyn and Samuel walked away. She sucked in a breath, struggling not to cry.

Clint reached out, resting a reassuring hand on the

small of her back, grounding her. His silent strength lifted her up, kept her from falling apart. How she'd missed it.

Missed him.

Blinking back tears, Daphne turned to Clint. "I'm happy for them, but I'll miss them deeply."

"I've missed...us."

She stared up at her husband, the man she'd left...for what? She couldn't even remember. Their daughter shifted beside them and Daphne glanced her way. She could talk to Clint later. Right now, they were due at the medical tent. "Ready?"

Mika nodded. Together, they headed toward the tent. After checking her in, due to space constraints the nurse requested that Clint and Daphne wait outside. Daphne began to argue, but Clint pulled her aside. "She'll be okay in there. Besides, it gives us a chance to talk. Alone."

She swallowed. Butterflies sprang in her stomach, fluttering back and forth. She might as well be Mika's age again, meeting a boy for the first time. She glanced at the tent and tugged her lip between her teeth. "Can you see her?"

Clint glanced inside. "Yep. She's sitting on a cot. A nurse is talking to her now."

Daphne exhaled. "I wish I could be in there with her."

"She'll probably be more forthcoming without us."

"You're probably right."

Clint raised an eyebrow and tilted his head.

"What?" Daphne almost laughed.

"I'm right? Haven't heard that in a while."

Daphne shrugged, trying to appear nonchalant. "People change."

He studied her for a long moment. "I'm proud of you, you know that? When I made it to your building and saw what you went through—" He shook his head.

"I wasn't going to give up on my family." She swallowed and wrapped an arm around her middle. "Not this time."

"You never gave up on us."

"Didn't I?" She turned away.

"Not on Mika, at least." Clint reached out and took her chin in his hand before gently turning her face back to him. "And I'm as much to blame about us as you are."

She swallowed and forced her gaze to stay level. "I'm sorry."

"So am I." He dropped his hand, but the feeling of his touch lingered. There were so many things Daphne wanted to say, but no words came.

"Would you—" He faltered.

"What?" Every fiber of her being waited, frozen.

"If we—" Clint cursed beneath his breath and yanked his ball cap up before shoving it back down on his head.

Daphne inhaled. She was the one who gave up before. The one who left without forcing the words out. She couldn't repeat her prior mistakes. She took a step closer. "I missed you, Clint."

His jaw ticked as he stared at her. "I missed you, too."

"I'd like to—" she paused a beat, but forced herself to keep going. "Try again, if you'd be willing."

Before she even finished the sentence, his arms were around her, pulling her close. His cheek was hot and scratchy against hers. "I love you, Daphne. Always have."

"I love you, too."

They stood like that, embracing, for a long moment. Until someone cleared her throat beside them.

Daphne opened her eyes to find her daughter standing there, one hand on a hip, face screwed up in a question. "You guys all right?"

She laughed and pulled away from Clint. "We're good, actually."

A faint hint of blush spread beneath Clint's week-old beard and he smiled at Daphne again. The sight of his face lighting up with hope and warmth and love melted something inside her. They might have been through hell this past week, but they made it out the other side.

And they would face whatever challenges lay ahead together.

CHAPTER TWENTY-EIGHT
CLINT

Clint stared out at the remains of their family home, mud coating the boots he'd managed to find at the only sporting goods store still standing near the Strait. The ground was thick and viscous. Mud and sloppy debris squelched as he stepped over remains of floorboards and wood siding.

The soft sounds of his daughter crying carried toward the house and he glanced behind him. Daphne perched on the edge of the rental car, Mika beside her. She stroked their daughter's hair as they both cried, Daphne's silent tears in contrast to Mika's louder ones.

He turned toward the sunset, a smear of pastel pink and sherbet orange across the sky. Mother Nature had an unbelievable capacity to be simultaneously beautiful and cruel. He stood in what he believed was their living room. A spot where he'd watched Mika take her first unassisted step—a wobbly toddle before she fell on her butt and clapped her hands in joy. Now there was nothing left but a muddy smear of carpet and a ragged chunk of wall.

For almost a week, they had been holed up in a motel room in one of the few nearby towns that had electricity and running water. A couple of days into their stay, they'd finally worked up the energy and the perseverance to scope out a local consignment shop and pick up a few clothing items. They weren't much, but they were clean and dry.

Clint had reminded Daphne and Mika that those things could, and would, be replaced all in good time, but to keep the faith and be patient. He'd been relieved when they'd both responded that all they cared about now was the fact that they were together, healing, and alive.

When they weren't sleeping or eating or talking in hushed voices about all they had endured, Clint had been on hold, pacing across the pine-colored carpet with a pay-as-you-go cell phone clamped to his ear.

He'd watched Mika read old paperbacks she'd picked up at the consignment shop, out of sheer boredom, just for something to do, something to help pass the time and ease the disquiet in her head. Clint knew about that disquiet all too well. The noise inside his head was a loud mess. He'd watched Daphne fidget and flip channels, her eyes on the TV, but not focused on what was happening on the screen.

They'd all been waiting for some news from the insurance adjuster. Clint on hold every day for a status update—everyone else, patient and listening. When the man finally got back to him with news, it had been bittersweet, but positive. If the house was deemed a total loss, the insurance company would cut them a check for the cost to rebuild and they could do that, or they could put the land on the market and move on.

Standing there, staring out at the destruction all around him, Clint already knew his vote. But he wasn't the only one entitled to a say. He glanced behind him again.

Mika pushed herself off the car and marched forward, the muck and mud sloshing beneath her shoes. She plowed across the remains of the lawn with determined speed.

"Mika, wait—"

"I just want to see what's left in my old room, Dad." She held up a hand to silence him. The hurt flaring in her eyes was enough to make him take a step back and let her pass. If she needed to see it, so be it. They would all have to process in their own way.

Mika eased past what Clint believed was the front of the house and stood in the rear, approximately where her bed used to be. On clear nights, when the town had gone to sleep, she would open her window and hear the water. Now, they were almost fronting the Strait.

Sure, the water had receded, but not nearly to its original level. At least four blocks of the town were permanently submerged. The entire Port was gone.

"Please be careful," Daphne called out to Mika as she made her way toward them.

Mika acknowledged her with a half-hearted nod and crouched to pick something up off the ground.

"What is it?"

"I can't tell." Mika shrugged and tossed whatever it had been away. She dug around a bit longer until she gasped. Bent over, Mika rummaged through the muck and pulled something from the remains of their home. It was rectangular and flat, and Mika used her shirt to wipe away the grime.

Clint approached her as she stood up. His breath caught in his throat. It was a picture frame. Inside was a photo of the three of them before Daphne left. He barked out a laugh laced with emotion.

"What is it?" Daphne called out, a few paces behind.

Mika wiped the glass, avoiding a crack down the middle. In the photo, the three of them stood on the beach, cool wind whipping Daphne's hair as she clutched Clint around the waist. Mika stood a bit in front, arms outstretched to take the selfie.

They were all laughing.

As Daphne stopped beside him, she gasped, too. Her hand came up to her throat and fluttered as she stared at the photo.

Clint's eyes stung with tears and a lump formed in his throat. He didn't believe in signs or miracles, not really. But this—this image of the three of them— preserved amidst all this chaos? It was something, of that, he was sure.

He glanced at Daphne. She stared up at him, eyes brimming with fresh tears. They might not be the happy, carefree family of the photo Mika still held in her hands, but they were together. They could be those people again.

No. Not the same.

Better.

He reached out and pulled his family in for a hug, Daphne on one side, Mika on the other. They stood like that for a long moment. Clint lifted his head and stared out at the destruction. The house across the street was gone, nothing remaining except the concrete pad and a cracked driveway.

A small yacht had washed this far inland, now beached fifty feet away. Two blocks over, a man picked through wreckage of what Clint assumed was his own house and his own pain. It would take years to rehabilitate the region. Years they didn't have to wait.

He cleared his throat. "The adjuster—he wants to know—"

"If we want to rebuild?" Mika's voice wobbled as if she were that little toddler again, unsteady on her feet.

Clint nodded against the top of her head.

"Do you want to?" Daphne kept her voice even, but Clint caught the hesitation.

"Well..." He dropped his arms.

Mika took a few steps forward and turned toward her parents, a hopeful look on her face.

Daphne pulled away. "What? What don't I know?"

Mika kicked at a broken hunk of wood. "We talked about some other options, but—"

"What?" Daphne's voice grew more confident, more insistent.

"We were waiting for you," Clint offered.

Relief flooded Daphne's face. "You were?"

He nodded. "What do you think about Boise?"

"Idaho?" Daphne raised an eyebrow.

"We thought it might be better for all of us if we started over in an area that wasn't so close to the coast."

"And was a bit bigger than Port Angeles," Mika added.

Clint held his breath, waiting for Daphne's reaction. He winced when she opened her mouth, expecting a protest, but none came. She seemed calm and surprisingly agreeable.

"I could be on board with that option."

Mika's eyebrows lifted. "Really?"

Daphne shrugged. "Why not?"

"That's it?" Mika still stared at her mother like she didn't believe her.

Daphne reached out and took her daughter's hand. "After everything we've been through, anywhere clean and dry is a step up. And besides, I like Boise. I had to go there for a deposition once. It's got this cute little restaurant district downtown with a few breweries. There's even a motel that's been turned into this upscale boutique hotel. It's weird and cool all at the same time."

"You mean the rooms don't smell like stale cigarettes and old French fries?"

Daphne laughed. "Not when I was there." She smiled up at Clint. "It was cute."

Clint exhaled a heavy sigh of relief. If Daphne was willing to relocate to Boise, maybe they really could all begin again as a family. He smiled at his wife and reached out a hand. Her face eased into a softness that warmed Clint's insides.

She threaded her fingers through his and turned back to the remains of their house. "We certainly can't stay here, and if I never see Bellevue again, it'll be too soon. So let's try Boise. Honestly, I don't care *where* we go as long as we're together. We survived. We made it through the biggest trial of our lives. Let's celebrate that we're still among the living."

Mika's cheeks blotched red, and tears welled in her eyes. She closed the distance between them in two strides and barreled into Daphne. She burrowed her head into her mother's chest, roped her arms around Daphne's waist, like she did when she was small, and cried. "That's all I needed to hear, Mom."

"It's going to be okay," Clint whispered, tears blurring his vision again. He enveloped his family in a huge bear hug. "We've already made it through the worst part. We can take the insurance money and start over. There's nowhere else to go from here but up."

18 months later

There are moments in a person's life that they want to hang onto forever. Core memories, that will last a lifetime, to carry and treasure.

This was one of those moments for Mika. She stood beside the podium on the stage, basking under the bright, warm lights in her new high school's auditorium. It was the week before graduation, but the celebrations for Mika and her family had already begun.

Tonight, she was being presented with an award for best overall student in the sciences department, achieving this accomplishment above every other student in her graduating class. It was a proud moment; one she'd worked hard to achieve.

Mrs. Cassidy spoke into the microphone at the podium, beaming with pride as if Mika were her own daughter. Head of the science department, Mrs. Cassidy had been a fantastic mentor. She'd encouraged her, helped her stay the course, and had given her pep talks when Mika's frustrations had threatened to get the better of her.

Now, after all these months of hard work, Mika stood on stage, waiting. There were other attendees, of course. Other kids who had done well and were receiving awards in their respective programs, spanning from math to theater and everything in between. But after the quake and the tsunami, science was Mika's singular focus. She stared out at the crowd and found her parents sitting side by side, her mother's hand resting in her father's.

She smiled as Mrs. Cassidy began to speak. "I can't think of anyone else more deserving of this award than Mika Redshaw. The best overall student in the sciences is quite an achievement, and Mika's hard work and dedication makes her the most deserving candidate to receive the award this year. Her science project involving wave dynamics and their implications in tsunami research not only won top place at the state science fair, but also helped her get accepted to Berkeley where she'll be pursuing a degree in geotechnical engineering."

Mrs. Cassidy paused for a moment, turning her head to beam at Mika. When their eyes met, the familiar sting of tears brimmed in Mika's eyes. Mrs. Cassidy took a deep breath and faced the crowd once again, steadying herself by pressing both her palms on either side of the podium's frame and squeezing it hard.

"Mika was one of the thousands of people who were impacted by the devastating earthquakes and tsunami that hit Washington and Oregon almost two years ago now. Her family was displaced. They lost everything. But she arrived here during her junior year, ready and willing to tackle all of life's challenges. It's been an honor to work with Mika, to prepare her for college, to help her reach her goals and achieve her dreams. I've never seen a more determined individual in all my years as a science teacher."

Mika was full out crying now, one of those embarrassing, ugly cries where her face scrunched and her cheeks flamed hot. Fat tears rolled, uninhibited, down her cheeks. She hastily wiped them away, but she couldn't hide her emotions—the combination of grief and pride that swirled inside her.

"It's been an honor to teach you." She slid a medal over Mika's head and an eruption of applause exploded through the entire auditorium.

The clapping and whistles and cheering went on for what seemed like several minutes. Mika stood there with her medal around her neck and her framed plaque cradled in her hands, searching again for her parents amongst a standing ovation crowd.

She spotted them in the center, standing the proudest and tallest among the rest of the parents. Her father was clapping his hands with abandon, and her mother's face was blotched red, tears glinting in her eyes. She caught Mika's eye, her face a prism of elation and pride.

Mika was glad to receive the honors tonight, but that wasn't what made her cry. The things she cared most about in the world weren't things. It wasn't this award or her college acceptance or her plans for the future. It was her family. She wished Hampton could be there, standing beside her, winning her own award as she tried not to cry and wreck her makeup, perfect curls bouncing as she grinned.

But Hampton resided only as a memory now, in photos on her phone and in a place deep inside her heart. Her best friend would have been so proud. She'd probably have teased her endlessly about the tears and shoved a bar of chocolate in her face to make her laugh. Mika smiled through the tears at the thought.

Her father reached his arm out and slipped it around her mother's waist. He pulled her close and squeezed her tight, the epitome of proud dad. Mika's mom clasped her hands together and steepled them under her chin, then a moment later blew Mika a kiss from the audience.

Mika's mom told her over and over, even to this day, how grateful she was that Mika and her father had refused to give up on finding her, that even through all the trials and disasters, that they hadn't quit, that they had charged forward, determined to find her against the odds and everything else that had stood in their way.

Ever since the quake, Mika took that same determination and channeled it into every facet of her life. She knew how lucky she was to be alive. How lucky she was to have a family. She would never take it for granted. Not for a single moment.

———

Thank you for reading *Fault Lines: Aftermath*. Subscribe

to Harley's newsletter to be notified when she releases something new.

www.harleytate.com/subscribe

———

In the meantime, if you are new to Harley's work and are interested in more, check out the *After the EMP* series:

If the power grid fails, how far will you go to survive?

Madison spends her days tending plants as an agriculture student at the University of California, Davis. She plans to graduate and put those skills to work only a few hours from home in the Central Valley. The sun has always been her friend, until now.

When catastrophe strikes, how prepared will you be?

Tracy starts her morning like any other, kissing her husband Walter goodbye before heading off to work at the local public library. She never expects it to end fleeing for her life in a Suburban full of food and water. Tackling life's daily struggles is one thing, preparing to survive when it all crashes down is another.

The end of the world brings out the best and worst in all of us.

With no communication and no word from the government, the Sloanes find themselves grappling with the end of the modern world all on their own. Will Madison and her friends have what it takes to make it back to Sacramento and her family? Can Tracy fend off looters and thieves and help her friends and neighbors survive?

The EMP is only the beginning.

————

ALSO BY HARLEY TATE

FALLING SKIES

Fire and Ashes

Thunder and Acid

Wind and Chaos

Escape and Evade

War and Survival

———

AFTER THE EMP

Darkness Falls (exclusive newsletter prequel)

Darkness Begins

Darkness Grows

Darkness Rises

Chaos Comes

Chaos Gains

Chaos Evolves

Hope Sparks

Hope Stumbles

Hope Survives

NUCLEAR SURVIVAL

First Strike (exclusive newsletter prequel)

Southern Grit:

Brace for Impact

Escape the Fall

Survive the Panic

Northern Exposure:

Take the Hit

Duck for Cover

Ride it Out

Western Strength:

Bear the Brunt

Shelter in Place

Make the Cut

NO ORDINARY DAY

No Ordinary Escape

No Ordinary Day

No Ordinary Getaway

No Ordinary Mission

Find all of Harley's releases on Amazon today: www.amazon.com/author/harleytate.

ACKNOWLEDGMENTS

Thank you for reading the final book in the *Fault Lines* series.

As I've mentioned before, a few liberties have been taken, especially with place names and other minor details in writing this novel. I hope you don't hold it against me!

If you enjoyed this book and have a moment, please consider leaving a review on Amazon. Every one helps new readers discover my work and helps me keep writing the stories you want to read.

Until next time,

Harley

ABOUT HARLEY TATE

When the world as we know it falls apart, how far will you go to survive?

Harley Tate writes edge-of-your-seat post-apocalyptic fiction exploring what happens when ordinary people are faced with impossible choices.

The apocalypse is only the beginning.

Find out more at:
www.harleytate.com

Made in the USA
Middletown, DE
10 October 2023